THE O'KEEFE EMPIRE

A Western Story

Other Five Star titles
by Jane Candia Coleman:

Moving On: Stories of the West
I, Pearl Hart

THE O'KEEFE EMPIRE

A Western Story

JANE CANDIA COLEMAN

Five Star
Unity, Maine

Five Star Western
Published in conjunction with
Golden West Literary Agency.

February 1999

First Edition

Five Star Standard Print Western Series.

The text of this edition is unabridged.

Set in 11 pt. Plantin.

Printed in the United States on permanent paper.

Library of Congress Cataloging in Publication Data

Coleman, Jane Candia.
   The O'Keefe empire : a western story / by Jane
Candia Coleman. — 1st ed.
     p.   cm.
   "Five Star western" — T.p. verso.
   ISBN 0-7862-1324-8 (hc : alk. paper)
   I. Title.
PS3553.O47427O38   1999
813'.54—dc21   98-42373

This book is for Glenn
with all my love

Acknowledgments

My thanks to John Tanner who educated me about Warner's Ranch and the Carrizo Corridor; to Lynn R. Bailey of Westernlore Press, whose book, WE'LL ALL WEAR SILK HATS, gave me the idea for THE O'KEEFE EMPIRE; the Arizona Historical Society which has preserved so many valuable diaries and recollections of those who actually made the drives from southeastern Arizona to San Diego; and, as always, to Glenn Boyer who gave me the title and the heroine and bore with me while I wrote.

Jane Candia Coleman
February, 1998

Chapter One

The man who boarded the train in El Paso had been staring at her for hours, and Joanna O'Keefe, choking on smoke and cinders and swatting flies, was nearly at the limit of her patience. She wished she'd had the sense to stay at home and wait until her husband came for her, instead of embarking on a journey comparable to a descent into hell.

Outside the open windows of the car the land stretched — dry, brittle, embroidered with creosote and here and there a field of nameless, tawny flowers on slender stems. In the distance she could see mountains, also nameless, and as foreign to her — raised as she'd been in the Texas hill country — as the surface of the moon.

In his letters Alex had described a lush valley — "high desert," he called it — but covered with grass for hundreds of miles and watered by a river and streams that formed in the mountains where oak and juniper grew. Had he been lying? Writing his dreams, blind to reality as he was apt to be? She shook her head in a small gesture of denial. Could he have lied to her about such a thing? No, he was her husband, her lifelong friend, and a wife did not think ill of her mate — or, if she did, she banished the thought before it grew into anger or the silence of despair.

That was how she felt now — desperate — with the blue eyes of the stranger watching her. An infant wailed somewhere in the car, the cry of a child who had passed the limits of frustration and refused to be comforted.

Comfort! It was four walls and a roof, and a cool breeze

skittering off the creek and through the pecan trees. It was Alex coming home for supper, full of talk and his usual dreams to share with her. She could see him seated across the table with its homespun cloth, his face lit by lamplight, his eyes sparkling.

"I've met a man, Joanna. A Scot. He's going West to make his fortune raising cattle. He's already found a place near the Mexican border, and the land is free for the taking. Think of it, my dear! Land! Freedom! Room to do as we choose, live as we've dreamed. There's money in cattle, and the range isn't crowded like here. And there's grass, empty range, and we'll be there first."

Those had been his words that day nearly two years ago. She'd heard him, and a shiver had run down her spine. She was the practical one, content within her house, the boundaries of the farm that had come to her when her parents had died. She knew the soil, the cycles of weather, the ways of crops and animals. And she knew her husband, that strange man with dreams always in his eyes.

Still, she had asked: *"Is there a town? What will you do on a ranch when you even hate farming? Won't it be much the same thing?"* And had seen his gray eyes harden to slate at the implied criticism.

"John McLeod wants a man with knowledge of the law, not a hired hand. We've spent the last week in discussion and have agreed. He and I will go out and get settled, and then I'll come for you. I've already promised money for our share."

"And you didn't tell me? Didn't even ask?" Her voice, soft but with the ring of steel, had echoed between them.

"Not until I was sure." He put his elbows on the table and leaned across it. *"Don't refuse me this, Joanna. I've made up my mind. This is our chance. I've never liked it here, never belonged. You know that."*

She had known. She had remembered when he and his father had arrived, remembered the skinny, wide-eyed little boy whom all the kids had mocked for his attention to his studies, and how she, feeling swift pity, had stood up to them, ten years old but sure of her own strength. She had stood in the school yard, hurling stones with deadly accuracy. *"Leave him be! You hear me! You're all a bunch of"* — she had struggled for the word insulting enough — *"pigs!"*

After that she had mothered him, the scholarly kid with the shiftless father. Some weakness in him had brought out the toughness in her, a ferocity that, as they had grown older, had turned to passion. He was hers, had always been. They both had known it and married in spite of the misgivings of her parents. It had seemed to her that each had what the other lacked and that, she told herself, was what their marriage was about.

"Do I get a chance to meet this man?" she asked, her voice heavy now with irony. *"This dream seller?"*

"It's not a dream, Joanna, and, yes, I want you to meet him. He can explain better than I can, so I asked him to supper tomorrow."

Her temper flared. Without a word, without discussion, the entire course of her life had been altered, and now she had to cook supper for the man responsible. *"Nice of you to tell me,"* she snapped, then regretted her irritation when she saw Alex's face.

"It's all right. I'll make do," she said. *Hadn't she always, and her mother before her? Hadn't she been the silent strength in their union — until now, with the coming of a stranger and his visions?*

Yet, in spite of herself, she was drawn into those visions. John McLeod, with the soft burr that made his speech alluring, and a practical streak that appealed, won her over by the time they'd finished supper.

"Land for the taking," he said, looking her straight in the eye. *"And a fortune to be made on cattle. The market is out there. The*

11

towns, the forts, the Indian reservations all want beef. The miners, too. What's needed are suppliers, and close at hand. The place I've found is made for cattle, so if they want beef, we'll give it to them."

It had made sense. Then. Now, looking out, she wondered if they'd all taken leave of their senses, if they'd come to this forlorn place only to dig their graves in the rocks and sand.

It had been months since she'd gotten a letter from Alex, months of loneliness and the fear she attempted to smother before it blotted out reason. Suddenly, after a week of sleepless nights, she had made up her mind. Her place was beside Alex, wherever he was. With typical determination, she found a buyer for the farm, packed the things she needed or couldn't bear to leave, and sent off a note announcing her arrival.

Now, with the arid land spread around her, the pale sky made paler by blowing dust, and the interior of the train car a smoke-filled oven, she wondered if she hadn't made an irrevocable mistake, cut her traces, left the overwhelming green of the hills for a seared plain, a husband vanished.

And all the while the stranger watched her out of blue eyes shadowed by the brim of his hat, a constant reminder that she was a lone woman, prey to advances in spite of the gold band on her finger.

He had never seen a woman as lovely as this girl in her dark green traveling dress and a bonnet that framed her face like a pair of cupped hands. He would have liked to ask her questions — who she was, where she was going — but he was a gentleman, and she, obviously, was a lady brought up never to speak to strangers even in a situation such as this where the rules could be eased just a little, formality dispensed with.

Damn, it was awkward, the two of them facing one another, knees almost touching, the silence like a glass wall between them, while outside the land seemed to move, empty, unshaped by human hands, challenging, like a dare. And he'd never refused a dare in his life. That was why he was on his journey — in response to a call for help from his brother. He was needed, a fighter like all the men in his family, and ready for whatever challenges there were to be faced in this new country.

He smiled to himself. Up to any challenge, was he? Why then hesitate to speak to his fellow passenger, regardless of the fact that she sat there guarding her virtue, refusing to meet his eyes, her shoulders set square under the green jacket?

The engine lurched. A cloud of smoke and ash blew in through the open window, and Joanna dabbed at her eyes that filled with tears, her courage finally blotted out.

Moved by the sight of her distress, he spoke before he thought. "Don't cry, lass."

Startled, irritated at the visible sign of her own weakness, she looked up. "I'm not."

"That's good, then." Her eyes were greenish, full of intelligence in spite of the tears.

"It's the smoke," she said. Having broken the silence, she was not willing to resume it. What, after all, could happen on a train filled with passengers?

He didn't disagree. "I've been wondering if your Columbus didn't feel like this in the middle of the ocean. As if he'd be sailing the rest of his life with never an end."

She looked out the window. Columbus, indeed! "I think I'd like the ocean better," she said with a shaky smile. Then her curiosity, which her mother had always prophesied would lead to trouble, got the better of her. "Your Columbus," he'd said with a familiar whir in his words like water running over stone.

"Where are you from?"

"Glasgow. In Scotland," he added, having met many without any notion of geography.

Her tears dried, as much from excitement as from the wind that blew in the window. "How odd. My husband's partner is from there. Maybe you know him. John McLeod."

He laughed, a great roar rising out of his chest that caused the other passengers to turn and stare. "I do, indeed," he said, smiling into her shocked face. "He's my brother. The youngest of us, come West to make his fortune in the cattle business. But he wrote saying there was trouble, and so here I am. But you. . . ." He hesitated as he remembered his brother's words: *Thieves, murderers, rustlers, and Indians, all taking whatever they want, killing whom they please, and no protection from the law.*

"It's no place for a lady," he said finally.

Her chin went up. "A lady's place is with her husband. I'm not afraid."

Perhaps she was foolish. Or courageous. Or a mixture of both. In any case, she was here, and it was too late to stop her, not that he could, with that determination written all over her face.

He shrugged. "Fear has its place."

"Perhaps. But there's no sense conjuring ghosts or worrying ahead of time."

Brave. And practical, too. He found himself liking her more than was proper, and she another man's wife.

"Hasn't your husband written to you of . . . of difficulties?" he asked.

"He said he'd found paradise. But that was months ago. I . . . I haven't heard from him for a while." She hated the admission, hated the fact that her voice shook.

The husband was either a fool or a dreamer, Angus

14

thought. Most likely a fool to let a young woman come into a land where murder was commonplace. Still, John had liked him well enough. **Steady** he'd written about Alex O'Keefe. **And with knowledge of the laws.**

"I hope it's all you expect," he said lightly.

His words, his attitude, irritated, as if he were ridiculing her, and who was he to do that, as innocent of the future as she was?

"I have no expectations," she answered shortly. "Only to be with my husband. For the rest, I'll deal with whatever happens."

He accepted her rebuke with a smile. "I, too. But, so far, everything has been strange. This country. It's so big. Anything can happen."

"And probably does." She smiled back, for hadn't she been thinking the same? "It's an adventure, Mister McLeod. I was trying to see it as one, anyway. Except for the smoke and the flies." She swatted her forehead, then rubbed her fingers on her soiled handkerchief. "I guess it's different from Scotland?"

He looked out at the red earth, rocks blackened as if scorched by fire, stunted trees with their frail, moving leaves, and was stricken with homesickness so acute he was, for a moment, speechless.

She read his face. "I know," she said gently.

"Do you?" He recovered himself. "And do you know that in Scotland at this time of year the sun scarcely sets before it's up again, and the lochs are as blue as the sky?"

"Lochs?"

"Lakes, ma'am. Deep water, and the hills around them prettier than a painting. And when the heather blooms, it's a sight, and none to match it."

In her mind she saw it — in opposition to the country be-

15

yond the window. Probably a fantasy but vivid, nonetheless. "It sounds lovely," she said.

"It is, ma'am. It is." He reached into his pocket and pulled out his watch. "And if I'm right, we've only a few hours before we get off and begin a real adventure."

"Here?" Looking, she saw a vast expanse of glittering sand, distant mountains rising blue and lavender. "It's . . . it's not what I thought," she stammered, the fear she'd denied earlier grabbing her throat.

Angus chuckled. "Not even my brother, who's a bit of an optimist, would have fallen for such a place. I believe the ranch is several days' journey to the south."

Irritation replaced her fear. A dreamer and an optimist, she thought bitterly, and her life in their hands. And with the sale of the farm she hadn't any place left to go. She'd cut her traces blindly, putting faith in a few words on paper.

Tears welled up again, but she forced them down. Self-pity was weakening, and she had never allowed it, nor would she let this man with the boisterous laugh and honeyed tongue see her unguarded. Keeping her head bent, she rummaged in her basket and pulled out two apples, handing one to him. "If that's true, we'll need our strength," she said.

His stomach wanted beefsteak or venison roasted over the coals, and a glass of good whiskey tasting of the bog to wash it down, but he accepted her offering and bit into it with good grace. From the beginning there had been women with apples, and men to eat them, even here, as far from home and civilization as he'd ever been. Still, he thought, there was something to be said for the mountains that rose at the farthest edge of vision, fading, changing color as the sun rose and began to descend, something poignant, a loneliness that struck to the heart as the dazzle of white sand they were crossing pierced the eyes.

16

One would never know all, he decided, never discover the secret places in those rocky barriers, never be able to grasp the splendor of the whole. He thought he might come to love this place with the same kind of love it was possible to have for a woman whose mind was her own, mysterious, alluring, and with that he glanced across at Joanna who, like him, was staring out, the look on her face indecipherable.

She caught him, smiled, the corners of her mouth turning up like a cat's. Then she said: "We might find beauty even here. Not your lochs or my trees, but something else. Something you can touch like those mountains. Earth's bones."

And with that speech, Angus McLeod fell in love:

Chapter Two

The station appeared like a mirage, distorted by heat waves that rose from the *playa,* a stretch of white alkali dotted with scrub grass. Two dust devils danced out across the plain without purpose or destination.

A lone man stood on the platform, a taller, thinner version of her fellow passenger. John McLeod. Joanna swallowed her disappointment. Where was Alex? Why wasn't he there to meet her, as eager as she? Perhaps he hadn't gotten her letter, and she wasn't expected. Now she would have to explain. Now she would be alone with these men on a journey of two days into the heart of this strange, echoing country.

"There's John!" Angus stood, balancing himself against the rocking of the car, and extended a hand to her.

"I don't see Alex." Her voice trembled. Something was wrong.

"Probably inside," he said, one part of him hoping it was true for her sake, the other hoping for more time alone with her.

She shook out her skirts and retied the strings of her bonnet. The year she'd been alone suddenly seemed like ten, and this man, this Angus, more familiar to her than her own husband. "You've been very kind," she said, suddenly formal. "Thank you."

"My pleasure." Foolish words! Foolish language that failed to convey any meaning but the superficial. In silence, he escorted her down the aisle and out to the platform where the sun caught them unawares.

18

"Missus O'Keefe!" John McLeod stood in front of her, his face registering shock and disbelief.

She squinted against the harsh light, felt her heart beating fast, faster.

"Alex?" she said, wanting to stop her ears, turn and run out onto the *playa* where the dust devils still danced their wicked dance. "Where's Alex?"

"My God," he said. "My God. Didn't you get my telegram?"

She forced herself to stay still. "No. I didn't get anything. Where's Alex?" she repeated, her voice rising.

"Come inside. Out of the sun."

But she was stubborn, proud in spite of her terror. "Tell me," she said.

He took both her hands. "He was on his way to town to file some papers. One of the hands heard shots. Whoever it was ran off and left him. He was dead by the time our man got to him." Without thinking, he'd blurted it out. Seeing her, somehow fragile in the glare of the sun, he regretted his hasty words, and his eyes darkened with sympathy.

Her head whirled like the dust; the sound she heard was her own keening, repressed, moaning in her ears. Yet, she didn't completely break down. Some part of her, the part that seemed like a spectator, was whispering: *You knew this might happen. He was so innocent. And he came here for you, because of you, hoping to make a home.*

Angus, as shocked as she, put a steadying arm around her shoulders. "My God, man, where's your sense? What kind of a way is that to break such news, and her so full of hope?"

"And what a way to greet your brother," John retorted. Then, more gently: "I'm sorry, Missus O'Keefe. Very sorry. You took me by surprise. We've had a run of trouble, and I've nae had my head on straight."

19

His eyes were bloodshot, and his face was drawn. In spite of her pain, Joanna took pity on him. "I understand," she said, though she didn't, might never. "An apology isn't necessary."

Again that spectator's voice rang in her head. *It's Alex who owes you the apology. He got himself murdered, probably because he refused to carry a pistol. He's left you, and now here you are with nothing to go back to. Nothing at all.* Oh, she'd warned him time and again. Even now a Derringer lay deep in the pocket of her skirt. Her father had taught her to shoot as a youngster, and she'd honed her natural ability. If only she had been here, perhaps Alex would still be alive.

She choked back tears. Crying on the platform was useless. Crying anywhere was useless. Alex was gone, and she was alone with these men she scarcely knew. Now she had, as she had feared, a trip of two days and after that a sojourn in an empty house alone with her husband's effects. But it had to be done. She squared her shoulders.

"Is . . . is his grave marked?" she whispered. She had to know that he had at least had a decent burial.

John nodded. "It is. And if it's any consolation, he didn't suffer."

She didn't ask how he knew, didn't want to be able to visualize Alex alone, dying, in the inhospitable vastness of this country. But somewhere out here was the man responsible, a murderer with no more respect for human life than for an insect crawling on the ground, a man she would like to see hanged. She curled her fingers into fists and felt her nails bite into her flesh.

"How soon will we be leaving?"

"Missus O'Keefe . . . ," John began, but she cut him off.

"Joanna, please," she said. "I suppose we're partners, now."

"I can't let you do this." He was frowning, horrified at her proposal. "The ranch . . . it's nae a place for a woman. It's not safe. You should go back home. I'll not cheat you, I promise you that . . . make sure you get your profits, if there are any. Alex was a good man, and I'm sorry to have lost him, to have had you come all this way for nothing." Damn! What kind of female nonsense was in her head?

"But I haven't come for nothing," she said, meeting his eyes to make sure he understood her determination. "I want to see my husband's grave, and, after that, I'll do what I can to help you. I was raised on a farm, and I'm not afraid of hard work. Besides, I don't have another home. I . . . I sold everything before I left." God! How could she have been so deluded? She'd been as bad as Alex, never thinking of the reality, only of their reunion.

Well, it was done, and she was here. She squared her shoulders. "It's quite simple," she said. "I'll have to take up where Alex left off, and hope I don't disappoint." Dismissing John, she turned to Angus. "Will you help me with my bags?"

In spite of himself and the situation, he smiled. Joanna was clearly a woman with her mind made up, and neither he nor his brother was a match for her.

"Cheer up, little brother," he said. "Help has arrived. Two fighting McLeods and one feisty woman can lick their weight in horse thieves."

"It'll take more than the three of us to keep from going under," came the dour reply. "The wagon's over there in the shade."

Joanna followed his gaze, saw a buckboard and two muscled mules, and gave a brief nod of approval. You could always tell the cut of a man by the condition of his animals, and these were sleek and in prime shape. It could be hoped that the cattle and horses were equally as well cared for.

"A nice pair," she said, hoping to bring him out of his dark mood.

"Yes," he agreed, then added: "I hope we can keep them a while. The Apaches like nothing better than mule meat."

Where was the optimism that she'd seen across her dinner table? This man was bleak, tired, walking a fine edge. Was that what life here did to one? Was that what it had done to Alex so he went to his death with a sense of relief? Clearly someone had to take charge.

"Stop it!" she snapped, startling both men. "I'm the one who's had the bad news. I'm the one whose life is over before it hardly started! Alex and I didn't even have a child, and there you stand whining about everything. If you'll pardon me, that's hardly the way to run a ranch or win a fight. And I intend to win this one with or without you."

She felt better when she saw shame and confusion cross John McLeod's face.

Chapter Three

She sat between the two brothers, dazed by the turn her life had taken, by her decision to stay where she was instead of going back to home and safety. But she had no home. That was the truth of the matter. She had nothing of any value, except a partnership in an unknown venture and her wits — such as they were. At the moment they seemed frozen, as cold and incapable of feeling as her heart. Without Alex she was rudderless, lacking a present and a future, and the men talking over her head, as if she were a sack of corn, inanimate baggage, deaf to their conversation.

Alex. The name was bitter on her tongue. She swallowed and sat, hands clutched in her lap, two halves of the whole that had been herself.

"They've cleaned up the worst of the gang," John was saying. "But only after they stole everything in sight, and the sheriff looking the other way and lining his pockets. 'Twasn't a secret, but we were all helpless. And we've still got the horse thieves and the Indians, damn their murdering hides. They come and go quiet as bogies in the glens. You'll find out. And I hope we live to tell about it."

"I've no intention of losing my hair to a red man or anyone else," Angus said with a look at Joanna. "And you're frightening the poor lass to death."

"It's not Indians I'm scared of," she said, pushing aside her misery.

"What then?"

She forced herself to sit straight. "Not knowing where I

am or where I'm going, and a horrible welcome on top of it."

John slapped the reins over the rumps of the mules. The last thing he needed now was a woman to look out for, even one as pretty as his dead partner's widow. And it had sounded so simple at the start — millions of acres to be had from the government, cheap Mexican cattle, and the markets crying out for beef. But that was before the cowboy gang had stolen him blind, before the Apaches had jumped their reservation again, holing up in the Sierra Madres and raiding as they pleased. Still, her last words were a reproach. "Missus O'Keefe . . . ," he began.

She interrupted. "Alex wrote me he'd found paradise. Now he's there, and I'm here."

John wished she wasn't. "You won't like it, if you'll pardon my saying so. We're a rough bunch."

That again! She looked around. In the long light of late afternoon the western mountains cast shadows across the valley, while in the east the smaller hills turned to gold. The track they followed was barely visible, winding through the yellow fringe of last year's grass and between dancing branches of creosote. Ahead she saw a formidable wall of rock worn by wind and water into turrets, spires, oddly human shapes. It was as if the gods had been turned to stone and stood imprisoned and silent, watching their approach.

They topped a rise and teetered, it seemed, on the edge of the world. Below them, a valley, grass-covered, shimmering, framed by more mountains, stretched itself like a great, undulant beast, southward into infinity. The word paradise came to her, and she understood suddenly — there was the infinite and the tangible — heaven and earth, one beginning where the other ended, and a part of this was hers by accident or design.

She put out a hand, as if to possess what she saw, and

leaned forward. Overhead an eagle, wings outstretched, rose on an unseen current of air, and its cry echoed that within her, spreading in ripples, echoing off rock. Paradise.

When she spoke, her voice was hushed as if she were praying. "I do like it," she said, seeking words for the dazzling vision. "It . . . it feels like home."

And that was truth. Here was her future, carved into mountain and valley, blessed by the voices of eagles, a gift she could not refuse, an emptiness waiting to be filled — with cattle, a house, and, though she could not say how she knew, with a great and enduring love.

She had the sight, Angus decided, watching the dance of light in her eyes, her outstretched hands. He wanted to ask her what was foretold there in the distant haze of the valley, what voices spoke that neither he nor his brother could hear. All over his homeland were women born with the sight, most of them snaggle-toothed crones, mumbling over a peat fire or peering into a cup while holding out a callused hand for payment. He'd always been a skeptic. The future, for him, proceeded from the present. What he did today influenced tomorrow, or so he had believed until now.

"What do you see?" he asked her.

She smiled. "Home," she repeated. "And happiness, though it's hard to believe."

And with that he had to be content, hoping that her vision, if that's what it was, included him.

"You never said you were living like a shepherd in a bothy," were Angus's first words as they pulled up in the ranch yard.

"And were you expecting Edinburgh Castle, maybe?" John had asked for help, but hadn't expected criticism, at least not so soon, and from his own brother to boot. "Out here, the cattle come first. Comfort has to wait a spell."

A spell! Joanna thought wildly, staring at the two adobe houses separated by a dogtrot. *I'm going to live in a mud hut and probably with scorpions in the walls, and I'm supposed to wait a spell! Not if I have anything to do with it.*

The yard was bare, worn down by horses, boots, the coming and going of ranch wagons. Beyond, she saw sturdy, high-walled corrals, a bunkhouse and blacksmith's forge where a horse stood cross-tied, pens for the chickens and a sow with her litter. Familiar sights and smells, like the farm, transplanted to the side of a small creek where cottonwoods danced. Like the farm, except for the miles of open range surrounding them. And on the hill the graveyard, rude wooden markers, a few names, and the largest, newest — **Alex O'Keefe, died, 1888.**

She went there first, her grief changed to anger. "Where are your dreams now?" she asked the mound of earth, and heard her words spin off and vanish before she reproached herself. Men had always died for their dreams, their beliefs. Alex had been no different. And now the dream was hers, a glimpse of something bigger than self, the seeds of power. And revenge.

Abruptly she stood up. The hem of her gown was dusty and covered with burrs. She would need shorter skirts, heavy boots, a hat like those worn by the men, and a decent pistol, not the Derringer in her pocket.

There was work to be done here, a business to make profitable. Her life depended on that, and so far all she'd heard were John's excuses. It was *her* husband who lay buried, *her* life that had been shattered. Therefore, it was her job to rebuild, take charge. And someday she would come face to face with Alex's murderer. She knew it, as she knew the feel of the hard ground underfoot, the heat of the sun that seemed to pierce through her skull.

And when it happened, she would shoot him down, leave him where he fell for the buzzards, the flesh-eating ants. She had been robbed not once but twice. It would never happen again.

The inside of the small house was dim. When her eyes adjusted, she saw a fireplace and hearth, a bed, Alex's trunk. And a woman by the hearth, a young woman, judging by her face in silhouette, the black hair that glistened even in shadow.

"Micaela!" John's tone was sharp.

The girl turned swiftly and surveyed them out of unreadable, dark eyes. When she stood, Joanna saw that she was heavy with child, cumbersome under the dress that was cut full and fell to her bare ankles.

Joanna looked up at John, startled to find another woman there. "Who's this?"

He hesitated a second only, then said: "A sad story. She was probably an Apache slave, but we're not sure. She's mute, or else has decided not to speak. Alex found her one day out in the hills and brought her back. I've asked around, notified the Mexican government, such as it is, but there's no telling where she came from or how long ago she was captured. And she can't . . . or won't tell us. The Apaches have been taking Mexican slaves for centuries, as you probably know."

"I do." Joanna nodded, then looked more carefully at the girl. "But she's only a child."

He sighed. "Obviously not. I let her stay, and she's useful. Does a bit of wash when the boys need a change of clothes. Cleans up after the cook. T'wouldn't have been right to abandon her."

"But it's no place for a woman, as you've been telling me.

27

Especially one in her condition," she added with a touch of sarcasm.

"Not for one such as yourself."

"I expect I'll do fine." She advanced toward the hearth and smiled at the girl who stared at her as if she were a ghost. "We'll do well together, won't we, Micaela?"

Without a sound, Micaela turned and ran, light-footed in spite of the burden of her belly.

Joanna looked after her. "What did I do?"

"Naught, lass. I doubt she's ever seen a white woman before. She'll come 'round."

But would she? The fear in the girl's dark eyes had been disturbing. And something else had flashed across her face in the second before she ran. To Joanna it had seemed like hatred.

It hit her then — weariness, as if her spine was melting and could no longer hold her upright. The journey had been long, she was overwrought and without the strength to sort out her emotions. She sat down on the edge of the narrow bed — Alex's bed, and his trunk at its foot. She wanted a bath, sleep — a week of sleep, so she wouldn't have to feel or think.

He'd been living among men too long, John thought, acknowledging his sudden compassion. She was a wee thing, young, and slender as a willow shoot, and he'd been hard on her. Too hard, as Angus had told him with characteristic bluntness. And her a widow only a few days.

"You'll want a wash and a proper sleep," he said. "I'll send the girl back with some water. Cold water, mind you, but refreshing."

"Thank you." It was all she could manage. The room whirled around her, and his voice was far away. She was asleep before he shut the door.

Chapter Four

She woke to find she'd slept in her clothes, although someone had covered her with a striped serape. Obviously nights were cool in the high desert. She shivered as she stood up, shook out her skirt, and headed for the water bucket that sat inside the door.

It was amazing what a long sleep could do. She felt refreshed, alert, ready to meet whatever challenges there were in her new life. She wanted to ride out and learn the land, meet the neighbors, although she understood the nearest ranch was ten miles away, and the nearest town was fifty. Some day soon she intended to meet the banker, the merchants, the people who held the power, who bought the cattle she'd seen grazing in the valley the day before. *My cattle!* she thought with a thrill. Marked with the ranch brand, the Circle MC for O'Keefe and McLeod. Only now she was the only O'Keefe left.

The smell of meat cooking made her mouth water, and she washed quickly, took down her hair and brushed it, then braided it in one long braid that hung to her waist. *Fashion had no place here,* she thought with a smile. John wouldn't notice, and Angus seemed to accept her the way she was, just as Alex had. She was a widow now, she reminded herself, mouthing the word in an attempt to make it into acceptable reality. A widow — and with work to do.

Outside a horse nickered and was answered by another. A man called to someone and received a reply in rapid Spanish. The workday here, as on the farm, began early. She opened the door and stepped out, stood for a moment watching the mountains to the west catch fire and radiate the early light. It was a phenomenon she would see many times in the years that followed, but, seeing it for the first time, her heart stopped in her breast, her breath came short in worship of mountain and valley. Would it always affect her so? If it didn't, if she got so wrapped up in responsibility and troubles, she'd kill herself. "And that," she said aloud, "is a promise!"

It was possible, she thought, to love the land with a passion greater than all else — a hopeless passion, for possession, even through ownership, was not possible. She could look at, breathe, and touch the magnificence, but that was the extent of it.

Frowning over the enormity of her sudden comprehension, she walked across the yard toward the corral where John, Angus, and the men she assumed were hired riders stood talking, cups of steaming coffee in their hands.

Angus, sensitive to her presence, turned immediately. "There you are, lass. Up with the sun."

"From the looks of it, I overslept," she answered with a smile. "Did I miss breakfast?"

He shook his head. "We saved the best for you, or rather Tino did. 'For the lady' he kept saying when I wanted a second helping."

"Then I'll have to thank him." The cook, she knew, was more important than the hands, on a ranch or on roundup. Poor food, or lack of it, led to grumbling and mutiny, although these men gathered in a circle seemed steady enough at first glance.

Since no one had offered to introduce her, she decided to do it herself, and, smiling, offered her hand to the nearest, a tall boy of no more than nineteen. "I'm Joanna O'Keefe."

He met her eyes, then blushed to his hairline, and grabbed for his hat. "Rain Keller, ma'am. And . . . and I'm sorry for your trouble."

His honest face brought everything back. She blinked away tears. "Thank you, Rain. You're very kind."

The man beside him spoke next. "We're all sorry, Miz O'Keefe. Anything we can do, you just say." He took off a battered hat. "I'm Scotty Yarnell, and this fella's Chapo. That's Mexican for Shorty, as you can see."

Chapo bowed. *"Señora."* His eyes were sorrowful, conveying what he couldn't say in words, in contrast to the last of the bunch, who was staring at her with what seemed to be cynical amusement.

Her chin went up, and she met his gaze head-on. "And you?" she said, keeping her tone civil in spite of irritation.

"Terrill Fox," he said, not bothering to remove his hat or give condolences.

"How long have you worked here?" She had, she knew, no right to interrogate him, but his attitude was such that he deserved it. *Was he the one who had found Alex?* she wondered.

"Long enough. Never for a lady boss."

Trouble. He was trouble. She knew it in her bones, in the tension in the small of her back.

"I see." She looked at John who should have been the one to make introductions and reprimand the cowboy, but who, instead, stood stiff and unmoving.

"I'm not hard to work for, Mister Fox," she said, since no one seemed capable of speaking for her. "And I'm not about to give orders without knowing the ropes. But you'll find I am a fast learner."

As she figured, he backed down. "I didn't mean nothin' insulting," he muttered, although the look on his face said the opposite.

Before she had a chance to reply, John intervened. Good hands weren't easy to find. You took whoever came looking for a job and hoped he either learned fast or had worked on a ranch before. Terrill was probably one step ahead of the law, but at least he knew one end of a horse from the other. And, now, here she was, the widow with her notions and sharp tongue, stirring up trouble first thing in the morning.

"You'd better get some breakfast, Joanna. Tino is a wee bit temperamental," John suggested.

She bit down on a retort. No sense arguing over a hired man's lack of manners. "Have coffee with me," she said. "And tell me what's to be done . . . how your days go. I want to be useful, but I can't until I know the routine."

He laughed. "We do whatever needs doing, fix what needs to be fixed, and something always needs fixing. I've learned that much. This morning the boys are going to cut out thirty steers I sold to the butcher in Plataville."

"That's the closest town?" Angus asked.

"It's the *only* town, and a sorry one it is. A robbers' roost, if ever there was one. But it's full of miners, too, and they all have to eat, lucky for us."

Joanna frowned. "You must have other markets."

There she went again, asking questions about things a woman had no business bothering with. He forced himself to answer politely. "You needn't concern yourself with that, lass. But, if you want to know, we ship twice a year to the big packers in Chicago and San Diego."

"By rail?"

"Aye. And here's Tino with your breakfast."

She smiled at the little man with the drooping, black mustache. "I'm sorry, if I kept you waiting."

"No, no!" Tino waved his hands and bowed from the waist. "It's an honor to serve the *signora*. And I am sad

32

for you, believe me."

She supposed she'd get over it — the jolt of pain that hit every time someone attempted to console her. There would be others — neighbors, those who had known Alex — but how many times must she hear the words and be reminded? How long did it take for grief to be buried and laid to rest? She searched for a response and came up blank. "Thank you," she whispered. "Everyone here has been very kind." With the exception of Terrill and the girl, Micaela, who was nowhere in sight.

"I have beef, biscuits, and beans," Tino said. "*Mi scusi.* This is not Italia."

How odd! To find someone from so far away cooking in this lonely place. "How did you come here?" she asked, distracted from her sorrow.

Tino raised bushy eyebrows. "By boat, *signora*. And then on my feet. I walk here from New York, and learn much."

To walk all that way. "You're a miracle!"

He shook his head. "No. I am only Tino. But I have *l'avventura* in me. The wish to see many things, many peoples."

"And have you?"

"In my country, they would not believe what I have seen."

The strangeness of her circumstances overwhelmed her once more. Here she was in a new place, almost a foreign one, surrounded by strange men of all cultures and pursuits, yet all of them had only one goal — survival and money enough to do so. Was that what drove everyone? She didn't know, but supposed it was true, as it had been of her grandparents in North Carolina, and her parents who had moved to Texas to better themselves, and now of herself.

The instinct of people was survival, of self and of the race. She mulled over her sudden insight as she sat down at the place Tino had laid and tried to cut into the piece of beef on her plate. It was lean and tough as the sole of her boot, and she chewed hard as she listened to John and Angus making plans to ride out with the men. She swallowed a particularly gristly piece and said: "I'd like to come, too. Is this our beef I'm eating?"

"It is."

"People really buy this?"

John stiffened. "Miners, soldiers, the reservations want beef. We supply it. I haven't heard any complaints."

"They'll eat anything, then," she said, and heard Tino stifle a sound like laughter.

John drummed his fingers on the table. "It's only a beginning. Mexican cattle are cheap. We buy them, put what weight we can on them, and sell them. There's a decent demand."

But for how long? The world was shrinking. Here was Tino from Italy, two brothers from Scotland, and out there, in the vastness of America, were cities filled with people, many of them wealthy and demanding the best. For how long would they put up with servings of gristle and tendon labeled *beef*?

She gave up trying to eat and rested her chin on her hands. "Listen," she said slowly, "I know what you think of me. I'm a woman, and women aren't supposed to get involved. So I'm in the way. But what I feel is this . . . and you can laugh if you want, but I'll say it anyhow. I've seen the new cattle. Texas is filled with them. I've even eaten the meat. What we're selling won't compete. Not in any market and not in ten years. We'll be out of business and this ranch will go back to wilderness. I don't want that, and I don't think you do. I've only been here for a day, and already I don't want that. We're all here to build something, but to do it we can't stand still and do nothing while the rest of the world changes."

John didn't answer for a long while, concentrating on lighting the pipe he'd pulled out of his jacket pocket. He'd come from Scotland where the stock was bred that was being imported to improve America's herds, but he hadn't expected a woman to assess their major problem so quickly. All the ranchers were concerned over the poor quality of their herds, and some had already brought in blood stock. He and Alex had merely tried to keep going until they turned a fair profit.

It was Angus who broke the silence. "Have you any idea of the cost of blood stock per head?"

"Probably about a hundred dollars for a good shorthorn bull. Not impossible, and others are doing it. I've just held off." John puffed his pipe, and the tobacco glowed. "You're both welcome to look at the books. I've spent carefully. The money's gone into stock. Cattle, good horses, then drilling wells, building this place, and paying the men. But we've lost a lot of horses, and God knows how many head of cattle. We couldn't afford that kind of loss, but I cannot stop the thieving, short of taking the time to track the thieves myself. There's those here who do, seeing as we've got no law to speak of. It's just" — he took his pipe out of his mouth and waved it — "there's only so many hours in a day, as you'll find out."

"And now?" Joanna asked.

"Now we're on the edge." He hated having to make the admission. It sounded like failure. Angus cleared his throat. His blue eyes were serious, yet there was a light in them, a steady fire that reached out to the others.

"Down, but not out, Brother. I've brought money from our dad, and some of my own. It'll help, I suppose."

"And I have what I got for the farm," Joanna added.

35

"We're in this together, so you won't be fighting by yourself any more."

John puffed a cloud of fragrant smoke that hovered over the table a moment, then disappeared. Thanks, humility, came hard to him, especially thanks to a woman he'd seen as a nuisance to be gotten rid of, but who now appeared as a savior.

"If you're both sure," he said, his Scots burr becoming more pronounced as it always did when he was pressed.

"We're sure," Angus said.

"Three heads are better than one, I think," Joanna agreed.

"I'll be seeing Colonel Harrington at the cattlemen's meeting next week," John said. "He's brought in good bulls from California and may still have some for sale."

The corners of Joanna's mouth curled in a smile. "No, John," she said gently. "*We'll* see him. I assume we're all going?"

Angus chuckled. She was implacable. All the more reason to love her. "Aye, John. Our money's as good as anyone's, and so is our presence at this meeting."

"But there's nae a woman in the lot!"

Joanna knew when she'd won. "There is now. And I'll be ready to ride in a few minutes, if you'll excuse me."

"And there's nae a lady's saddle on the place!" John got out.

She grinned at that. "I'm no lady, John. I'm a farmer's daughter used to riding bareback. Any saddle, any horse'll do."

She walked away. Behind her she heard Angus's voice filled with laughter. "You've met your match, John. A wee lass with her mind made up. Give in. There's no man on earth ever won out over a determined woman."

John's reply was muffled, but she didn't care. She'd made

her point and had found a champion. For sure she'd find others. The prospect cheered her. One solution to the emptiness in her heart was work, and she'd never turned her back on even the most difficult job.

She pushed open the door to her room and stood still, too stunned to move or cry out.

Chapter Five

ner point and nad found a dc... line of
The error was covered up... One solution to... and there...
to see here was... on... and then down through her body as
with the door all...
She had...
signed to never...

Micaela was kneeling beside her trunk, the contents tossed on the ground around her.

"How dare you touch my things!" Joanna flew across the room and grabbed the girl's shoulders. Didn't she have enough to worry about without protecting her property from a half-witted child who'd gotten herself in trouble?

Micaela froze, defiance in her eyes, and, although Joanna's first impulse was to slap her, she held back. Probably the girl had enough rough treatment, had perhaps even been raped.

"Get up!" she commanded. "I won't hurt you." And when Micaela didn't move, she pulled her to her feet. Then she saw the photograph clutched in the girl's hand. Her own wedding photograph taken in Fredericksburg. There she was, radiant, holding Alex's arm, while he smiled down at her in the way she'd always loved.

With an aching heart, she snatched it away and dragged Micaela to the door. "Don't dare!" she shouted, past caring who heard. "Don't dare touch that!"

"Joanna, for God's sake, what's the matter?" John came at a run, with Angus close behind.

"Don't 'for God's sake' me!" She was still shouting over the rawness of her loss. "Keep her out of my things. She has no right."

Tears ran down Micaela's smooth cheeks, but she made no sound, and they upset John for a reason he couldn't verbalize. Instead, he turned on Joanna. "You've scared her half

38

to death, and over what? Not much, I'll wager."

Joanna caught her breath, heard herself screeching like a mad woman and over the simple curiosity of a peasant girl. "She was going through my trunk. She had my wedding picture." The fact choked her, and she swallowed hard. "It's all I have left of him. I . . . I can't have her stealing it."

"I see," he said, although he knew Micaela wasn't a thief. "I'll make sure it doesn't happen again." He patted the girl's shoulder, and she looked at him, emotion plain in her eyes.

"Do that." Still clutching the photograph, Joanna went inside, buried it under a pile of clothing, then closed and locked the trunk and put the key in her pocket.

"What was that about?" Angus asked John as he watched Micaela running toward the wash house. "She's scared out of her wits."

"So would you be, and that woman screaming her head off. And the trouble won't stop there, mark my words."

"Why not?"

"It's not a happy tale." He walked over to the corral where five horses stood tied. "What I'm going to tell you is between us and no other. Agreed?"

"Of course."

"She was taken by Apaches. Used by them and then kicked out. O'Keefe found her, half dead. We took care of her. There wasn't anything else to do. But, when she recovered, she fastened onto him. Wouldn't let him out of her sight. And one night he found her in his bed, or so he said. I believed him. Still do. But now there's a bairn, and who knows who it'll take after, or what's to be done when she finds out. We'll hear some screaming then, I'd guess."

Angus stood frozen, one hand on the neck of the horse nearest him. "Joanna," he whispered.

"Aye. Joanna. The betrayed wife . . . God help us."

"She loved him," Angus managed to say.

"And he loved her, I'm sure. But what's a man to do, and a woman warm in his bed? You tell me."

Angus couldn't. All he saw was Joanna and her imminent pain. "Send the girl away," he said. "Get her out of here."

"I did. She came back. This is home to her, or all she knows as home. Joanna's the same, but she has a right to be here. It's not enough to have problems with rustlers, Indians, the damned weather. Now we've got woman trouble, and make no mistake, it'll be woman trouble."

It would. Of that Angus had no doubt at all. "Maybe I'll get an idea," he said, although he doubted it.

"And it's between us, remember."

"Of course." Certainly he wasn't going to be the one to break the news and shatter the lass's belief. What kind of a man had he been, this Alex O'Keefe, to betray a woman like her? If she were his — but she wasn't. Might never be, thanks to the fates who even now seemed to be conspiring against them.

They followed the creek westward around the southern end of a chain of rugged mountains, Joanna, Angus, and John, with Scotty, Chapo, and Rain, ranging on either side. Here was another valley, as wide as a delta, running north and south, its limits lost in a haze of heat.

"Mexico." John gestured with his chin.

Angus followed the motion, saw a spill of yellow grass and more mountains, purple and forbidding against the arch of blue sky, and, for the first time, he realized the problems facing the ranch and his brother's dream. Beyond an invisible line lay another country, another culture with many languages, and mountains that were home to renegade Indians and thieves who cared for nothing but the pay-off.

He pulled up his horse and sat staring into the distance, a distance that eluded definition. Joanna stopped beside him, her chin set in a firm line, her hands resting on the broad horn of the Mexican saddle that she rode astride, like any man and with a man's confidence.

When at last they looked at each other, it was with awe, a sense of their own smallness.

"It's as big as here," Joanna murmured.

"You'd need an army to go into those hills," Angus said to John, who smiled grimly.

"Aye. And not an army to be found. They captured Geronimo and now don't care about whoever else is down there. The Mexicans have no arms, and their soldiers aren't interested. So we sit here and give our stock away to the takers. The Apaches, Mexicans, thieves from wherever they've sprung from."

"You'd need a thousand men just to patrol the border." Joanna assessed the situation with new-found vision.

"At least."

She squinted off, her eyes shaded by the brim of the floppy hat Tino had given her. Problems — and a dream shared by many. Somewhere was a solution, and she'd find it. "Let's go look at cattle," she said.

Seeing them, she wished she hadn't. Bony, thin by Eastern standards, wild as rabbits, they took to the brush as Scotty, Rain, and Chapo attempted to cut out the thirty head destined for the local market. Without warning, a steer wheeled and charged her, picking up speed as it came.

"*¡Ciudado!*" Chapo's shout came a second before her horse gathered itself and bolted. Horsewoman that she was, she kept her seat, glancing back over her shoulder once, then reining up, when the steer lost interest.

"Are you all right?" Angus fought the fear that shook in his voice.

"Guess so. These critters are dangerous." She didn't mention the fact that her heart was pounding like a hammer.

He replayed it in his mind, saw certain disaster — the animal's long horn hooking horse or rider, and Joanna helpless on the ground. *His Joanna.* "Madness!" he exclaimed. "Look at them. Uncontrollable, worthless beasts."

"And our fate rests on them. For now," she reminded him. "Thank God, there's men willing to take on the job."

"The sooner we replace them the better," he muttered. "You might have been killed."

The excitement over, she had time to think back, see it happening, and her heart lurched again. Except for the quick reaction of her horse, she might, indeed, be dead, or at least seriously injured. Still, what she'd faced was what these men faced every day. Danger, too, was a part of this new life, and she would have to get used to it.

"A close call." John rode up. "Now you see why I worried about you."

His constant fussing stiffened her spine. "I'm tougher than I look. And this is a good horse." She patted the neck of the well-muscled bay whose instinct had saved her.

"He is that. I bought fine horses on the advice of a Texan I met. Steel Dust and Shiloh blood, if that means anything to you."

Her passion had always been horses, from the huge draft animals on the farm to her own team, broken to harness and saddle. "You had good advice," she said. "Everybody in Texas knows about those two. I'd like to keep this one for myself, if you don't mind."

Her approval, after all that had happened, was pleasant, and she looked very much at home mounted on the bay. He leaned back in his saddle. "Of course. And tomorrow, maybe, you'd like to ride out and see the breeding stock. I've a stallion and some fine mares I've managed to keep safe. So far."

At last she'd found common ground with him. "I'd love to. Angus" — she turned toward him — "will you come, too?"

"I'll follow where you lead, lass," he said, his voice still roughened by his earlier fear. "Just ask me."

She heard it — concern, the barely hidden edges of something more, and deep within she responded with excitement, the beginning of a road that opened in what had previously been a wasteland. Unable to conceal her pleasure, she flashed him a brilliant smile, then dug her heels into the bay and let him run as he'd been wanting to do, as she'd been wanting to do, with the wind, the weight of the past left behind in the dust, the shimmer of light, the long shadow of the thrusting hills.

Chapter Six

Plataville rose from the earth like a malignant growth. Tents, tar-paper shacks, stores hastily nailed together, and adobe buildings dotted the desert like mushrooms after rain. In the heat of summer, the town appeared like an ugly mirage that could be destroyed by a cloudburst or a gust of wind, and Joanna blinked in surprise as they rode down the dusty main street and were assailed by the clamor of a mining boom town. Never before had she noticed the difference between country and city, but the unaccustomed racket, the shouting, laughter, music from the dozen or more saloons unsettled her.

Most women on farms or ranches looked forward to their visits to town, but already she longed for the silence of the valley, a silence so deep it was almost tangible. Only necessity had brought her here with Angus and John, and Rain driving the wagon.

The Cattlemen's Association meeting was to be held in the Grand Hotel. There were questions she wanted to ask, bulls to bargain for, other ranchers to meet. And in her pocket was a list of supplies given to her by Tino, and another list written by herself. It said: **boots, .44-40 Winchester and same caliber pistol, material for riding skirts, blankets, and clothes for baby.** For, in spite of her initial anger, Joanna was worried about Micaela and the unborn child.

She supposed she'd have to be with the girl when her time came. At the thought, a shiver ran down her spine. If anything went wrong, she'd be helpless, holding two lives in her uned-

44

ucated hands. She'd brought farm animals into the world, but never a human. Still, it couldn't be much different. She was planning to see the doctor for advice before she left town.

She was relieved when they stopped in front of the hotel. No sense worrying about what might never happen. The present was what was important, and what could be learned in this rag-tag town from those who held the future of ranching in their hands.

The hotel lobby was cool and dim compared to the brilliance of the street, but, when her eyes adjusted, she was amazed at the splendor of what had appeared as another poorly constructed building. Red-flocked wallpaper covered the walls, a crystal chandelier hung from the ceiling, and comfortable chairs were placed at intervals around the room next to tables, holding newspapers and magazines.

"It's so grand," she said to John. "I didn't expect it would be like this."

He gave her a quick smile. "We have some comforts." Then he turned, hearing his name called.

"Henry. Good to see you." He shook hands with the dignified gentleman in a well-tailored suit and polished boots. "And may I introduce Joanna O'Keefe. Colonel Harrington."

The Colonel was a tall man no longer young, but distinguished, with a well-trimmed beard and a pair of steel-blue eyes. His handshake was firm. "My pleasure, ma'am. And my sympathy for your loss."

She'd expected it. Nonetheless, sorrow swept her. "You're very kind," she murmured.

Harrington kept his grip on her hand, assessing her beauty and what he sensed was a quick intelligence. A breeder of fine horses and cattle, good blood always interested him, and here it was in the shape of a clear-eyed young woman.

"You'll be joining me for dinner, I hope."

"I intend to. And to come to the meeting. I'm a partner now with lots to learn."

"Wonderful!" He beamed at her. "Sometimes I think we're just a bunch of stick-in-the-mud cattlemen. New ideas are what we need."

"Even from a woman?" she asked lightly.

He tightened his fingers around hers. "My dear, I've always believed that it's women who do the thinking, and men who carry out their plans. Never mind the opinion of the rest of the world."

"Then we should have a very interesting evening." He was flirting with her, of course. She knew that with a kind of thrill in her own womanhood. Perhaps there was an advantage in being female, and unmarried, regardless of what he'd labeled the "opinion of the world." She withdrew her hand and smiled. "I look forward to this evening."

He nodded, keeping his eyes on hers. "I, too."

So that was the way it would be, John thought. One smile, one upward glance out of those green eyes of hers, and every rancher in the territory would be her slave. She'd have her say, and God alone knew what the result would be. And here was Angus glowering at the back of the departing Harrington as if he'd like to go a few rounds with him.

"Steady, lad," John cautioned, and earned an equally dour glance.

"Who the devil is that? The laird of Arizona?"

"He might as well be. He owns the biggest ranch in our county, no question. And money's no problem for him, either. He'll hold on, even if the rest of us lose our skins."

"I'll not lose. Not my scalp, my skin, or that piece of ground you think is quaking like a bog under our feet. Nor anything else, either." *Certainly not Joanna.*

46

John read his thought. "Will you never learn?"

Angus signed the register, picked up his bag, and started for the stairs. "I've learned enough to know when I need advice and when I don't."

Joanna, who had walked across the lobby to take a closer look at a painting that had caught her eye, came slowly back, and was startled when Angus brushed past her without a word.

"He's angry," she said, puzzled.

"Nay, lass. Merely annoyed."

"Why?"

John bent and picked up her bag. "It's the way men are sometime. You'll have to get used to it."

He sounded as cross as his brother looked, and she resisted the impulse to shake him. She was glad she'd been pleasant to the Colonel. At least she'd have him to talk to at dinner. With a sigh she followed John up the stairs.

Joanna looked down the long table at the men who made up the association and repeated their names to herself. The Edwards brothers, Phil and Lem, farmers from Pennsylvania who had come West to make their fortune. Their 2E Cattle Company bordered the Circle MC on the north. Mellen Deering, gray-bearded, gray-eyed, owned the Artesia Ranch and land in Sonora, and bordered them to the east. Zeke Russell had a smaller parcel in the mountains, as did the Forsythes, father and son.

Colonel Harrington, seated at her right, dominated the group, but all were serious and determined, directly involved in their business, their livelihood.

With dinner over, they reached for their cigars, then looked at Joanna who understood instantly. In any other place she would have left them to their smoking and discussion, but she had no intention of missing anything that was said. "Please smoke, gentlemen," she said. "My father and my husband both did, and I find it pleasant."

"A rare lady, indeed," the Colonel said with approval.

"My presence shouldn't disrupt anyone's comfort."

Mellen Deering leaned across the table. "Will you be looking for a place to live in town?" he inquired. "My Clemmie's here, and she'd be happy to help you look. And happy to have another woman to gossip with."

Did he, too, want to be rid of her, or was he merely making polite conversation?

"I'll be living at the ranch, Mister Deering. It's my home," she said softly, and waited.

He stroked his beard a moment, wishing Clemmie would reconsider her feelings for the ranch and for himself. "And a rough one," he said. "I'm sorry for what happened. We all are."

The Colonel interrupted. "May I bring this meeting to order?"

The others nodded and leaned back in their chairs, giving him the floor. He cleared his throat, and, like a good actor, paused a moment for effect before he began. "Originally, we had proposed the writing of a bill to present to the legislature, pressing for stock detectives to patrol the border. This will still be a matter for discussion. However, as you know, I recently returned from a trip to Chicago where I heard a rumor that the meat packers, in conjunction with the railroad, were conspiring to raise the price of shipping cattle between here and California."

He paused again, saw that everyone's attention was focused on him, and continued. "I paid an informal call on the freight agent, a Mister Scully. He confirmed the truth of the rumor. The price of shipping our cattle to San Diego is to increase to more than one hundred and ninety five dollars per car, gentlemen. A price we can't afford to pay and continue in business."

There was a stunned silence following his speech, as each man figured profits and losses and came out on the short end.

"It'll finish us," John said. "California's been our major market all along."

"Our range is overstocked right now," Lem Edwards put in. "If I can't ship, I'm done for. Might as well drive 'em all back to Sonora and let the Injuns have 'em."

"Is there bargaining room?" Deering wanted to know. "Is this an empty threat?"

The Colonel shook his head. "I'm afraid not. The big meat packers want control of the market, and with refrigeration they'll get it. They can ship packaged meat at a quarter of what it costs us, and it's not longhorn beef they'll be shipping. I'm afraid we'll be forced to pay what they ask."

"Free enterprise has always meant putting the little fellow out of business," Angus said suddenly. "But it also means we can fight back for all we're worth."

"How?" All eyes turned to him.

"Is there no other market? No other way to get cattle to California?"

Joanna grasped his concept immediately, remembering the trail drives she'd seen — thousands of bawling cattle moving north out of Texas to markets that spanned the continent — living rivers of flesh, bone, and profit.

"We can drive them ourselves," she blurted, then felt foolish as they waited for her to continue.

"I'm . . . I'm not familiar with all this country," she went on, "but surely it's been done. Surely cattle have been driven to California before. How else did they get there?"

The Colonel blew a cloud of smoke. "Of course. I've done

it myself in the reverse. Brought in blood stock out of Oregon and California. It's possible, but only if there's adequate water. A Spaniard named Farges, and another, De Anza, did it about a hundred years ago. So did the Butterfield Stage and Kearny and Cooke."

She was fascinated, as much by the man's confidence as his knowledge. "Who're they?"

"Juan Batiste de Anza was a Spaniard. He marched an army, a bunch of settlers, a herd of cattle, and probably some sheep and goats to California. And they survived. Kearny and Cooke were Army officers. Cooke went through with the Mormon Battalion in 'Forty-Six. They made it through, but Kearny died in California. For another reason, of course."

At that, the comments burst out.

"It's not possible!"

"The cattle'll die of thirst before we get halfway."

"Crossing the Colorado's risky. And the ones that make it across won't make it through the dunes."

"The losses will be more than we can stand."

Did no one want to try? Or to think of an alternative? "So we sell out and go back to where we came from?" she asked, her voice rising above the objections. "We give up without a fight, and everything we've worked for is forgotten?"

John shot her a horrified glance. "It's nae possible to do what you're suggesting."

Harrington cleared his throat, looking annoyed. "I know from my own experience and from the facts of history that it is, indeed, possible. Even sheep were herded over that trail before the war. But what we need, before making a final decision, is a look at the routes, and there are several. We also should learn the availability of grass and water during each season."

Zeke Russell raised a callused hand. "My dad drove to

50

California from Texas in the 'Sixties. Still talks about it. I'll see what he remembers, and mebbe he's even got a map somewheres. But hell . . ." — he darted an apologetic look at Joanna — "beg pardon, ma'am . . . we all know it's been done once we think on it. And no railroad or big Chicago money's going to take what I have, and that's a damned promise."

"Good man!" Angus applauded. "As far as I'm concerned, I'm with you for however long it takes, whatever we have to do."

"I'll second that." Mellen Deering slapped a large fist on the table. "It's past time we, out here, stood up to the damn-yankees."

Joanna raised a hand. "If we do it, *when* we do it, will we all go together, or would it be better to go separately?"

Harrington nodded. He'd been right from the first. She was a clever, thinking woman. "A good question. Does anyone have an answer?"

"Small herds have a better chance," Deering said. "Especially if water's a problem."

"It'll mean some of us'll have to hire extra help," the older Forsythe put in.

"What's small?" Joanna wanted to know.

"A thousand head. Maybe less. And staggered, so there's graze for whoever comes next."

Zeke Russell frowned suddenly. "One thing. My dad's always telling about how that drive was dry for a good eighty miles, but I'm not sure how he crossed. He's always tellin' how when those cattle smelt water they ran off. Nobody could hold 'em. Couple hundred head went over a bank and died. Something to think about."

"There's losses on every drive," Deering said. "Damn' critters are unpredictable, even after they settle down. You got to count on luck, but the fact is, the way it looks,

51

we've got no choice."

"We'll have to make a decision before the fall gathering." Harrington had been sketching a rough map. "De Anza went around the Algodones dunes into Mexico, then turned north. The Butterfield Stage used the same route to Warner's Ranch, and, from there, it's only a couple days drive to San Diego. I assume we all have California contracts to fill?"

A look around the table gave him his answer. There were contracts and now no profitable way to fill them.

"Are we in agreement then?" He waited while each man assessed the difficulties. One by one they nodded.

"Good. We'll settle the particulars later." Harrington shuffled his papers. "Now I've brought a draft of the petition we were going to send to the legislature."

He went on, and Joanna let her thoughts drift. What they had decided sounded easy, almost simple. Gather cattle and drive them to market. But to believe that was to delude herself. The cattle were wild and dangerous, and the country to the west was, in all probability, as barren as that to the east. Of course, there would be losses. The question was, would there be profit enough to offset them?

It occurred to her that the meat packers both in Chicago and California were actually in control of the market, and without facing any of the hardships of the ranchers. It seemed a far better business than ranching and certainly less risky. The ideal situation would be to own both branches, to sell to themselves, and alleviate the middle man.

Her eyes narrowed as she pondered the idea. For the time being, she'd keep it to herself, ask questions, learn more, and, when she got to San Diego, then she'd see what her next move would be. Because, for sure, she was going along on the drive, and no one, not John, not Angus, not the devil himself, was going to stop her.

Chapter Seven

Clementine Deering, a small woman dressed in the latest fashion, came with her husband into the dining room where Joanna had just completed the purchase of six shorthorn bulls to be delivered by Harrington within the month.

The Colonel looked up. "Here's Deering and that woman he married," he said, his disapproval plain.

"You surprise me, Colonel." Joanna followed his glance.

"I've surprised many," he responded, getting to his feet. "It's good business practice. Keep that in mind. Now, if you'll excuse me. . . ."

"Coward," she murmured with a smile.

"Business, my dear. I have already had my pleasure for the morning." He extended his hand. "Missus Deering. Mellen."

Clementine gave him a slight smile, then, ignoring him, turned to Joanna. "You must be Joanna. I've been hearing about you from everybody."

Joanna refrained from meeting Harrington's gaze. "Good things, I hope. Have you had breakfast?"

Clementine swooped into the empty chair. "We have. We're early risers."

And why not? Who would want to lie in bed with this woman who reminded her of a parrot — beady-eyed, sharp-nosed, dressed in purple silk with a green-feathered bonnet? How could a man like Deering have married such a woman?

"My husband tells me you're actually living at your ranch," she began. "Believe me, you'll be better off to live in

53

town. I can help you find some place suitable, if you'd like."
That said, Clementine leaned across the table as if inviting
confidences.

Joanna risked a glance around, hoping Angus had come
in, or even John. Deering himself was talking to one of the
Forsythes, two tables away. No help in that direction.

"Missus Deering. . . ."

"Please call me Clemmie. Everybody does."

"Clemmie" — she took a breath — "the ranch is home. I
like it there. John has been struggling alone and needs help.
You must know how that is."

"I've been at the ranch. And I'm happier here. Let the men
do it. Let them deal with the troubles."

To Joanna's astonishment, the woman's eyes filled with
tears. "What is it? What's the matter?" she asked, distressed
without knowing the reason.

Clemmie crumpled the handkerchief she pulled out from
her purse, fingers working nervously, clenching and un-
clenching. It was a minute before she spoke. "We had a
daughter. She was just three, and lovely. So lovely. I took her
out for a visit. I was lonely, you see, and young enough to
miss my husband. So we went. And somehow . . . I don't understand . . . she . . . Lavinia, that was her name . . . wandered
off." She raised the handkerchief to her eyes for a moment
and struggled to gain control. "You've seen it. That land out
there. You know how it is. A child could be anywhere. Or an
Indian."

Joanna recoiled at the thought of what she was about to
hear. "Please," she whispered, "don't upset yourself."

"Upset! I have a right! I'll never forget. Never. Or forgive,
either." Clemmie's voice dropped to a hiss. "It was nearly
two days before we found her. She was alive. She said . . .
'Hold me, Mummy' . . . just before she died in my arms. I've

never gone back, and I never will. Let Mellen live there and risk himself. He's a hard man. A hard man. And I . . . ? I have no daughter, or ever will, if I have my way." Eyes closed, as if she were seeing it all again, she sat, a woman turned to stone by tragedy.

"I'm sorry." Joanna realized the inability of language to express grief and compassion. How many times had those words been said to her? How many times would she herself be forced to say them? "My husband. . . ."

Clemmie's eyes snapped open. "Your husband was as foolish as the rest."

"I beg your pardon."

"You'll find out, and, when you do, you'll come to your senses. You'd just better hope it isn't too late."

She was beside herself, Joanna thought. "Please . . . ," she began. "I loved Alex. He wasn't any more a fool than you or I."

"All men make fools of themselves sooner or later, and your Alex wasn't any different," Clemmie snapped. "You'll learn."

The woman was crazed. Nothing she could say would help or make a difference. Joanna pushed back her chair and stood. "I'm afraid I have to go," she said. "And believe me, I feel for you in your loss. I hope . . . I hope we'll be friends in spite of everything."

Without waiting for a response, she ran through the lobby and out onto the board sidewalk where the traffic from the street, the music that had seemed threatening the day before now seemed a proclamation of life, the determined pushing of mankind upward and out of darkness.

Unsure of what to do, she stood watching a train of burros laden with firewood follow a Mexican woodcutter down the middle of the street, their small hoofs raising puffs of dust

55

that rose into a cloud.

Early though it was, someone was playing a piano in the saloon a few doors away, and playing it badly enough to make Joanna put her hands to her ears. *Damn the woman! What had she meant, saying those things about Alex?*

"Joanna. What's wrong?" Angus was next to her, looking at her, concern in his eyes.

"Nothing. At least nothing I can put a finger on. It's just . . . Clemmie Deering told me the most awful story. And then she . . . she hinted that Alex had gotten into some kind of trouble. I thought she was out of her mind, that, if there was anything wrong, John would've said something. He would have, don't you think?"

She looked at him, worry plain in her eyes, in the frown line that appeared between them. *Did everybody in the county know, then?* he wondered. *And if so, how long could they keep the secret away from her?* He sighed. "Pay her no mind, lass. Misery always looks for company."

"But she sounded so . . . so sure."

He reached out and took her arm. "She's an old biddy. And if I remember rightly, you had shopping to do."

She nodded gratefully. "Come with me?"

"I've already told you. Anywhere."

She heard it again, more clearly this time — a longing in his voice like the echo of thunder in the hills.

"I'll just get my list. I'll only be a minute."

Was Clemmie Deering right? she wondered as she climbed the stairs. Or was she merely hearing meanings where there were none, succumbing to fantasies with Clemmie and then with Angus? Everything was so new. She'd have to go carefully until the ground was steady underfoot, until her loss had healed over and she was herself again.

It had been almost a month since her arrival, a month of

shock and desperation in which she'd been moving like a shadow of the old Joanna, holding grief in abeyance. That was the only way she knew to go on, and clutching at straws had no place, at least not yet.

One by one, the valleys welcomed her home, opening their broad, golden arms, offering blowing grasses, the sweetness of late-blooming mesquite and hidden flowers. Mounted on the little bay, one with the smooth rhythm of his walk, Joanna knew a sudden joy at it all, a joy dispersed, when she saw Scotty coming toward them at a full gallop.

"Rustlers!" he shouted. "Run off five mares and colts last night, and headed right across the line."

Joanna did a quick tally. That left them with only ten mares and the gray stud, a costly blow.

John's shoulders slumped. "You see?" he asked, staring at the ground. "You see what we have to fight?"

Angus felt a surge of anger. He'd come prepared for trouble, and now he'd found it. The ranch was as much his as anyone's, and someone had dared steal what belonged to him. It wasn't to be borne.

"I'm going after them," he announced, "and devil take the bastards. We'll go home and change horses. Are you with me or no?"

"I am." Scotty fell in alongside. "And Chapo, too."

"And if you don't come back, if the thieving rascals blow off your head, what then?" John demanded. "Then there's just me and the lass, and a battle we'll lose for sure."

Angus's eyes were blue slits in his tanned face. "I'll be back," he said shortly. "Count on it."

And it fell to Joanna to stay behind, powerless, fighting her fears, going on as best she could, doing the ordinary things that women always did while the men went out and risked their lives. Perhaps Clemmie had been right, after all, and John. Perhaps they were all fools in search of some chimera that danced on the horizon.

She slammed a fist on her saddle horn. "Welcome home," she muttered. "Welcome back to trouble."

And there was plenty of that.

Chapter Eight

Tino met them in the yard, his face twisted in anguish. "*Signora,* it's the girl. It's her time, and I . . . I am only a man."

Joanna dismounted and stood holding the reins. "When? When did it start?"

He shrugged. "Yesterday, but maybe before. She make no noise. You come now, please."

"Get me some hot water and strong soap. And some clean rags, if you have any." She hadn't had time to see the doctor in town. Now she was wracking her brains as she gave orders, trying to remember what would be needed. "In the wagon . . . I have blankets and things for the baby. We'll need them later. I'll go and change and come right away."

What to do? A labor of a day and a night was already too long, and her knowledge was slight, confined to calves and lambs. And now she'd not have a moment to wish Angus a safe return. What were horses compared to the lives of men? Angus was her friend, her support. If something should happen, she'd be fighting on her own. Abruptly she squared her shoulders. Even thinking such a thing could bring bad luck. Besides, she had no time to dwell on it. Micaela lay in childbirth, the outcome of which was in her own hands.

She went to her trunk, unlocked it, and took scissors and a ball of string out of her sewing basket. *No need to relock it now,* she thought, scrambling to her feet at the sound of hoofs outside.

Chapo had brought three fresh horses out of the corral. Canteens of water and narrow bedrolls were tied on each sad-

59

dle, and Chapo carried a sack filled with the bare necessities for the trail. Angus was fitting a Winchester rifle into the scabbard when he saw her standing in the doorway — a picture to take with him, a woman to come home to, though she didn't know it, a wronged wife on her way to deliver her husband's bastard.

"Wish me luck, lass," he called.

"I do. Take care. Come back safe."

"I will, just for the sight of your pretty face." He swung up onto his horse, hiding his emotion with activity.

"Don't risk yourself," John said. "I need you more than horses, and that goes for all of you."

Angus raised a hand, stole another look at Joanna, then wheeled his horse and followed Scotty and Chapo out across the creek and onto the faintly marked trail to Mexico.

Joanna watched until they were only a cloud of dust, with John beside her, frowning.

"They'll come back," she assured him. "I feel it."

"Have you got the sight, then?"

"Whatever you call it. Sometimes it's like I hear things in my bones."

"I wish I could believe you."

"Whatever you believe is up to you," she said.

"*Signora*, you come!" Tino waved from the cook house.

She ran across the yard and into the kitchen, found Micaela on a cot behind the iron stove, a Micaela who, seeing her, drew back her lips in a silent snarl like a wild thing filled with rage.

Joanna knelt beside the cot and put a hand on the girl's head. It was cold, but damp with sweat. "It's all right," she murmured. "I'm here to help, if I can, and I hope I can."

Even as she spoke, a tremor wracked Micaela's body, and she opened her mouth in a silent scream.

It was the silence that made her agony so unbearable, her inability to find relief in even a whimper, and she had lain here alone all night trapped by innocence and pain.

Joanna drew a deep breath and raised the girl's skirt, hoping that birth was imminent. What she found were sweat-stained, filthy thighs, a gaping darkness, the scent of blood that made her gasp and stagger back. She had seen animals, but never a woman, not even herself. Was this how it was then — dirt and stench and the tearing apart of that most secret of places?

Over her shoulder she called to Tino. "Bring me warm water and soap and something to wash her with."

Sooner or later, this was what happened, whether by love or accident. You were reduced to sodden, helpless flesh while the new life, trapped in the cave that was body, was determined to exit.

Well, at least she could make Micaela clean. She ran back to her own room for a fresh shift and the bundle of baby clothes. If she had not been here, if she had never come, Micaela would have struggled alone, and no one on the place able or willing to help. No wonder they all said women belonged in towns in the company of others of their sex.

But that was taking the easy way, and she had always been a fighter, different from other women, tougher than most, although her instincts were feminine. She had chosen to remain here and so would face whatever came. She trotted back across the yard, intent on whatever lay ahead.

"How is she?" John was, as usual, worried. The whole situation was uncalled for, and in a way he held himself responsible.

"Not good. I'll do the best I can."

"That's all anyone can do."

"And hope it's enough."

Inside, she sponged Micaela who lay as before, snarling, but too weak to fight off the attention. And there was still no sign of a child. Joanna wiped her own face, and felt sweat running down her body. The heat from the stove and from the July sun, beating on the metal roof, was intense. *Didn't it ever rain?* she wondered. *Didn't nature have any mercy for its own? And how much more could Micaela stand?*

"Push!" she hissed as a contraction shuddered through the girl. "Push!"

The pains were increasing in intensity, and with each one Micaela's eyes rolled in their sockets, and she grabbed at the quilt with desperate fingers.

"Harder!" If this was how it was, Joanna was glad she'd never borne a child, regardless of the fact it would have been Alex's. It might have been herself lying here, attended by a woman equally as helpless as she felt, or by no one at all.

She pulled the quilt away and saw the crown of the child's head, reddish curls plastered tightly against its skull. Whoever the father was, he wasn't Apache. Not with hair that color.

"Just a little more. Push now," she said gently, laying a hand on Micaela's belly. "And whoever he was, I hope he was kind to you."

Micaela squeaked, a mouse caught in its death throes, as the next contraction pushed the infant's head further out.

"Once more!" she urged. "Once more. . . ." She looked up to see that the mother had fainted. Well, she'd pulled her share of calves when the mother was past pushing. Whether or not it was the same with humans, she didn't know, but something had to be done. "God help me," she whispered, then rolled up her sleeves, carefully grasped the tiny head, and pulled. There were the shoulders, perfectly formed, the slippery torso. She swallowed hard and pulled again, and suddenly a child lay gasping for breath in her hands, a girl-child, small but perfect, and with a crowning of wet, red hair.

Her hands went on by themselves, tying off the cord, lifting the infant in her arms, and cleaning its nose and mouth as any mother animal would do for its own. When she'd washed and wrapped the baby in a blanket, she turned to Micaela who lay still, a grimace painted on her face. She laid the baby on her mother's breast, then, frightened, felt for a pulse. She found none, only the cold rigidity of death. The enormity of the situation swept her, knocked her backwards on her heels, and at that moment the baby gave an anguished cry.

"Is it over then?" John and Tino stuck their heads around the stove wall.

"It's over," she said slowly around the lump in her throat. "It's over for Micaela, anyhow."

John's face twisted. "Dead?"

Joanna nodded. "But she has a baby girl. A little red-headed daughter. We'll never know who the father was, but he wasn't Indian."

John swallowed hard, wondering if it bore any resemblance to Alex, or if, indeed, it was possible to detect at this early date. "Now we'll have the raising of her."

What he meant, Joanna thought with sudden clarity, was that *she* would be responsible, that *she* had been catapulted into motherhood without knowledge or desire, and that the ranch would revert to the men while she stayed home nursing an infant not her own. An infant who needed her, she realized, as the baby turned, seeking a breast, and her arms automatically tightened around the fragile but demanding child.

Chapter Nine

"Hell of a thing, nearly gettin' ourselves killed to get milk for some half-breed bastard!" Terrill took another dally of his rope, tightening up on the hind leg of the cow with a twisted horn and murder in her eye.

Rain didn't answer. He was concentrating on keeping his own loop around the cow's horns, and keeping his distance at the same time. It made for slow going, her stretched between the two of them, but it was better than being charged by the maddened mother out to protect herself and her calf. He swung a leg at the little one that was running circles around them and bawling for its supper. Then he said: "We can't let the kid die. Miz O'Keefe'd skin us alive."

"If she knew whose bastard it was, she wouldn't."

"I ain't tellin' her."

"You ain't got guts enough."

The cow stopped suddenly, three legs planted in the sand. Rain was glad of the excuse not to argue. He could never win an argument with Terrill. Besides, he didn't want to talk about the boss lady or the mess her husband had gotten into. It was a nasty business, and her doing her best in spite of it all.

He spurred his horse, and the rope around the cow's head stretched taut. At the same time Terrill gave her some slack. She stood a minute, assessing her chances, then charged straight at Rain. Terrill dallied again, yanking her leg back, and she stopped, shaking her horns and bellowing.

"This'll take us all week," Rain said.

"Beats hearin' that brat yell."

Rain thought he'd rather hear a baby than the constant bleating of the calf and the bawling of its mother. One thing for sure, he wasn't going to be the one trying to milk the old girl. He grinned to himself. Whoever tried was going to get a hell of a lot more than they bargained for.

She bawled, she twisted her bony body into knots, she charged at anything that moved or didn't, aiming her good horn at whoever came near the pen where she and her calf were shut up.

In spite of himself, John was laughing. He'd never thought of the difficulties involved in milking a range cow. Now he thought it might be impossible, and, inside, the bairn squalling from hunger.

"Well, lass," he said. "Here's your dairy. Do you have a suggestion as to how we go about it?"

"None." Joanna looked at the others. "Anybody know?"

"She must be tied, *signora*," Tino offered.

Terrill turned away so they wouldn't see his contempt. Had they thought it was going to be easy? Why had they come here anyhow, these dudes and their whores? He spat out the taste in his mouth, remembering Micaela.

Rain shook out his loop. "I'll head her . . . tie her horns to the snubbing post. Terrill . . ." — he shot a look at the man sitting, shoulders hunched — "you heel her. Keep that leg out of the way. And somebody pen up that dang' calf. The rest is up to whoever wants to try." For a minute he was embarrassed, telling everybody what to do like he was boss. But hell! The kid needed food, and all of them standing around dim-witted like a bunch of birds on a branch.

On the farm Joanna had had milk cows, two of them, both placid creatures who came in the morning and evening and stood calmly while she milked. For sure, one of them had had an ornery streak, but nothing like this enraged and terrifying bundle of energy that fought every attempt to subdue her, snorting, slobbering, twisting like a dust devil.

"Permesso?" Tino held out his hand for the old pail, and Joanna gave it to him gladly.

Slowly he approached the cow, who rolled a baleful eye in his direction. He began to talk, slowly, calmly, and kept talking as he laid a firm hand on her shoulder. She shuddered, pulled against the ropes, and snorted loudly, but Tino kept talking. After a time he knelt down and cautiously began to milk, disregarding the sounds of rage that came out of her, the slap of her filthy tail in his face.

"What's he saying?" John was perplexed.

"Who knows? But it seems to be working."

"Aye. For now."

Yes, Joanna thought. *For now.* But, for the next six months, they'd be going through this every day, one more task piled on top of all the others, a duty she hadn't asked for and didn't need. Except that the child's life lay in her hands, and life in any form was precious. At that moment, she'd have given years of her own for a decent milk cow.

She had never been so tired. The baby cried incessantly, for food, for warmth, out of discomfort, and it was up to Joanna to figure out why, when all she wanted was sleep and the sight of Angus and the boys coming up the trail. Why that was so, she didn't know, only that it was true, and that, at the same time, if someone would offer her a ticket back to Texas, she'd take it, give up the insanity of bringing the ranch to prosperity, an orphan to adulthood.

None of the men seemed interested in the baby, and Terrill, whose very presence grated on her, had suggested, while sitting high on his horse and heeling the cow, that she

66

drown her like an unwanted kitten. Even now the thought and the man disgusted her.

She sat in a rough chair under a mesquite tree, the sleeping infant in her arms, and tears slipped down her face onto the child's head — tears of frustration and exhaustion, of pity for herself and all of them struggling in this brooding valley for no reason other than a dream. Finally, she closed her eyes and slept, and, although the sound of hoofs penetrated her sleep, she did not awaken when Angus rode in, tired, filthy, as much in need of sleep as she. Seeing her, he sat still in shock and wonder.

It was the dapple of sunlight on her hair, and the curve of her arms around the child that put him in mind of a madonna — gentle, compassionate, caring. He'd fallen in love with her for reasons he realized now were superficial — because she was pretty, bright, and good company. But seeing her with the lines of weariness giving her face a stern dignity, he understood the strength of the woman, the courage that had brought her and kept her here in spite of loss, danger, loneliness. And she must be lonely with only John and himself and a bunch of rough hands for company, along with the mute peasant girl whose ignorance had brought about the child that threatened all of Joanna's beliefs. Damn them all for a pack of barbarians! Himself most of all, running off in search of horses and with some vision of adventure, and leaving her to fend for herself.

He dismounted and walked toward her, and she, sensing a presence, opened her eyes.

"You came back," she whispered, conscious of the sleeping child.

"I said I would. And what do I find? You mothering someone else's brat. Where's Micaela?" He spoke harshly, irritated with the lot of them.

67

"She . . . she's dead. I didn't know how to save her."

"So now you've taken responsibility. Again. It seems to be a habit with you, lass. Is there nae a wet nurse anywhere?"

She stared at him. "I never thought."

"Aye. Well, now I'm home, I'll do the thinking. You're worn out. It's written on your face, and it's thanks to us men and our selfishness."

She lifted a hand to her cheek, then let it fall. "She cries so much."

"Bairns do. But you're not her mother." Except she might have been, damn O'Keefe's philandering soul.

"The horses," she said. "Did you find them?"

"Only two mares. Scotty and Chapo are bringing them." Best not to talk about what they'd gone through, the misery of the country and the journey, the foals dead among black rocks, already stinking and fly-blown, and overhead the buzzards, hundreds of them that they'd had to beat off with their ropes. The mares were standing guard, refusing to leave until finally they'd been roped and dragged. Mothers again! And here was Joanna squeezed into a mold she didn't fit.

"That's good. I'm glad you're back. I was worried." Her eyes fluttered shut, and she slept again, peacefully this time, not even waking when Angus plucked the baby out of her arms and took her to the cook house.

"Give the lass a rest, for God's sake," he ordered Tino. "She's worn out. Is there no one here who gives a hoot but myself?"

Without waiting for an answer, he went in search of his brother.

Mellen Deering rode in just before supper. He'd stayed in town an extra two weeks, hoping to make things right between himself and Clemmie, but she'd wanted none of it —

or of him. A bad business. He shook his head sadly. A man wanted a loving wife, even if she was living away from home. He wanted a woman to talk to, companionable, understanding. Clemmie was none of those things. Not any more. Not since the tragedy. His own little girl. He could see her still in his nightmares, see Clemmie's face as they buried her in the unrelenting ground.

"Mellen!" John startled him out of his reverie. "I thought you'd be home by now."

"I had things to see to." He pulled his saddlebags off the saddle. "And I thought we needed to talk about this trail drive."

"It'll take a lot more than talk."

The baby's wail cut through the evening.

"What the hell's that?" Mellen asked.

"Micaela's bairn. She died in the birthing, and Joanna's being mother. Between rustled horses and a cow to be milked, we've had a time."

"This is no place for a baby." Mellen spoke around his own poignant memories. "Leastways, not without its real ma. Best take it to town and find a nurse. There's lots of Mexican women with babies who need money." He heard himself and caught the glimmer of an idea. "Clemmie'll be glad to help."

John assessed his neighbor with compassion. Like everyone else, he knew what had happened, had witnessed Clemmie's selfish sorrowing. "Supper's nearly ready," he said, side-stepping an answer. "Come on in."

"And I'm hungry. But seriously, you can't keep a baby out here. There's too many risks." Seeing Joanna, he broke off and removed his hat. "Missus O'Keefe."

"Mister Deering. You're just in time to eat with us." If the baby would give her a half hour, she thought, smiling grimly.

"I hoped I would be. Everybody knows Tino's the best

cook around. And what's this about you trying to take care of a baby?"

She spread her hands. "Somebody has to. She's all alone."

"But not here. I just suggested to John that you take her to town and pay a wet nurse."

Her face brightened, then she frowned. In spite of it all, she'd grown fond of the tiny girl with her crown of red hair and dark blue eyes. The helplessness of the newborn had awakened some latent desire in her, a hunger for something of her own. Still, she'd been making do with a pap-rag soaked in the cow's milk, when she knew the baby needed more and better nourishment.

"And it might be a good thing for Clemmie," he added, seeing Joanna's hesitation.

But Clemmie was half mad. Hardly the perfect choice to oversee a child. "I'll think about it," she said.

"You'll do more than that." Angus had made up his mind as soon as he'd heard Mellen's idea. "I'll take you back to town myself in the morning."

"So soon," she protested.

"Not soon enough. This is a ranch, not a nursery, and we've business to attend to."

"And that's why I stopped by," Mellen said. "I did a little investigation, and this trail drive's not only possible, it's a necessity. The railroad's raising its shipping price within the next few months. That'll take care of any profit we figured on from the fall roundup. If you think it's a good idea, I suggest that you folks and I pool our cattle and our hands, and we take off for California as soon as we can after gathering. If we're first on the trail, we'll at least know there's good grass."

John chewed on the stem of his pipe. "It's a good point. And if we don't push too hard or too fast, they might even put on some weight."

Joanna looked at him in surprise. He actually sounded eager. "Let's talk over dinner," she suggested. "Mister Deering, you'll spend the night, I hope?"

His eyes twinkled. "Thought you'd never ask. Sleeping on the ground gets harder every year, though I guess I'd better get used to it. There won't be any beds between here and San Diego."

The hugeness of the project struck her. Although she'd been the one to suggest it, the hardships, the gritty reality had not surfaced. But if she went along, as she fully intended to do, there would be no place for a child and certainly little chance for that child's survival.

With that she made up her mind. "I'll go to town in the morning," she said to Angus.

He heard her resolve and laughed to himself, understanding her reason and wondering what his brother and the rest would say when they, too, understood. A woman on a drive — more awkward than even this rough outpost. Well, he for one would be glad of her company. She'd make the long road bearable.

Chapter Ten

"Why come to me with this . . . this bastard?" Clemmie stood in the door of her house, hands on her hips, glaring at Joanna, Angus, and the baby.

Angus stepped forward, barely controlling his anger. "Because we had faith that you'd help us. Help the bairn who's not at fault for how she was born, bless her. She only wants a chance at life, and you, being the good Christian woman that you are. . . ." He let his words dwindle, choking over the unmerited flattery.

"At least, we thought you could tell us how to find a nurse," Joanna added quietly. "She's hungry, you see."

"So are we all." Clemmie leaned toward Joanna. "Who does she take after?"

"Not Micaela." Joanna pulled the blanket away, exposing the shocking red curls that, surprisingly, had not fallen out but had taken on new luster.

"God help us!" Clemmie stepped backwards like she'd been shot, and Joanna lost the slight grasp she'd had on her temper.

"Never mind," she snapped. "Forget we came. I'll . . . I'll leave her on the church steps, poor thing. Or take her to the prostitutes. I've heard they have kind hearts in spite of everything."

"What?" Clemmie's voice rose and cracked. "You mustn't! You can't! I won't let you do such a terrible thing. Give me my baby!" She snatched the bundle from Joanna and hugged it to her bosom. "Kind hearts, indeed! You should be ashamed, yes, you should. As it is, you're lucky. This poor child certainly is. The girl who works for me has a new baby. She's a good girl. Trustworthy as far as it goes, and cleaner than most. Married to a cowboy who comes home just long enough to start another, and she puts up with it." Clemmie's mouth pursed in disapproval. "She'll do it . . . for the money. Leave the child, and, if you're smart, you'll forget about her and go on about your business. Better for everybody that way."

Blast the woman! Angus thought. *She was a walking, talking machine!* "We'll decide that later."

"What's her name? I suppose she's not even baptized."

Joanna looked stunned. "I forgot. It all happened so fast, and I didn't know what to do, except what I did."

"I told you. It's no life out there."

"You did." She contemplated the sleeping girl. "Call her Allegra," she said after a minute. "There's enough sorrow in her world."

"Allegra, is it?" Clemmie bent her head, and, as she did, the newly named infant opened her eyes and seemed to be looking directly at her. "Heavens! Such a serious little thing!" A smile began at the corners of Clemmie's mouth.

Angus and Joanna exchanged glances, as the older woman cooed. "Hungry? I bet you are. And wet, too. Well, don't you worry. Aunt Clemmie's here now, and you're safe. Prostitutes!" She looked up at Angus and Joanna and snorted, then turned back to Allegra. "We'll have you fixed up in a minute, and not a fallen woman to come near you."

Joanna leaned over and kissed the soft cheek. "I'll be back," she whispered.

"Stop fussing! And bring her things inside," Clemmie snapped. "She'll be fine with me. And if you had any sense . . . ," she stopped, shaking her head. "Never mind. She's in good hands."

"I know." In spite of everything, Joanna felt a tug at her heart. Quickly she went down the steps to the street. "If we start now," she said to Angus, "we'll be home that much sooner."

He raised an eyebrow. "And here I was about to escort you to a fine dinner at the hotel."

She pictured it — the two of them in clean clothes at a table covered in white damask, a bottle of wine, and talk flowing easily. But not yet, she told herself, avoiding complicated reasons. Not yet.

She put a hand on his arm. "Someday we'll do it, but not now. Let's just head out."

And that meant camping out one night, and no baby to keep her occupied, nothing between them but the shadow of a dead husband and the laws of propriety.

"How about when we get to San Diego?" he asked, trying to turn disappointment into humor.

She stopped walking. "How'd you know I was planning to go?"

"Because anybody who's watched you knows how that mind of yours works, lass."

"The others . . . they'll try to stop me."

"And have as much chance as trying to catch water in a sieve."

She chuckled at the analogy, then looked off to the mountain barrier, one of two between them and home. "Am I being foolish? They all think so. Even Clemmie. But it's my life. My gamble. I want to see the drive succeed. I want to help push it through, not sit home, worrying."

He pulled her around to face him. "I won't stop you. Since we've neither of us ever done such a thing, we'll have to stick together. Learn together. And it'll be a grand adventure to tell our grandchildren when we're too old to do anything but

74

sit by the fire. When the world's changed, and what we did is history."

What did he mean . . . *our grandchildren?* She decided not to press the issue. "Making history," she said instead. "I like that."

"We all do it one way or another. Some is written, some is only tales passed on, but all of it's true, written or not. Think about that."

She would. Never again would she look at her surroundings in the same way. The ranchers, the rustlers, the Apaches in their mountain hideout, the valleys themselves, all had a history, and she, Joanna, was part of it, might one day be a larger part, her name in books, her exploits remembered.

"Angus McLeod, I think you're remarkable," she said, giving his arm a squeeze, then setting off in the direction of the livery stable as fast as her feet could take her.

Angus moved the mules at an even trot over the pass and down onto the floor of the next valley, keeping a wary eye on the storm clouds building in Mexico. All the talk had been of drought, of another dry summer, but, from the looks of the sky, that was about to change, and the two of them without shelter.

Joanna sniffed the wind like a dog, scenting rain before it reached them. In all the broad valley nothing moved except a few buzzards riding a thermal high overhead, circling fearlessly on black wings.

They found the freshly killed cow five minutes later, or what was left of her — haunches hacked off, entrails spilling into the dust. Automatically Angus pulled up, sickened at the wasteful slaughter.

Joanna risked a glance around, saw nothing, but instinct and the tracks of unshod horses in the dust told her. "Keep going," she whispered, reaching for the shotgun beneath her feet. "Just move."

"Who'd do such a thing?" He was bewildered and furious.

"Somebody hungry," she said grimly. "Probably Apaches. Go on!"

"It was one of our cows." He was still angry.

"And we've got thousands."

"Generous, are you?"

Was he turning into his brother? Was he going to sit and argue, when their lives possibly hung in the balance? "We'll be lucky to get out of here, if those Indians are still around. What's your life worth? Whip up those damn' mules."

That got through. He flapped the reins, and the mules moved out. "More than one bloody cow," he said. "Where are the devils, do you think?"

She surveyed the brush from under her hat brim. "Close, I'd guess. Or maybe we scared them off. For now," she added, resting the double-barreled shotgun across her knees. She wanted to be home, behind walls with necessary reinforcements. Instead, they were here alone, danger lurking in the folds of the ground, the stands of mesquite. In all the heat-shimmering, cloud-shadowed emptiness they had only themselves to deal with possible and sudden death, because, to the Apache, they were the intruders, part of the white horde that had taken their homeland, instigated terror, caused hunger and disease.

Angus had talked about history, and here it was — here the consequences of conquest, real, not imagined, the stuff of nightmares. She said: "We're the enemy. I never thought I'd be that. I never thought how it'd feel being the hunted."

He knew. His whole beloved Scotland had been more than once turned into a killing ground. The old names rolled off his tongue — Bannockburn, Culloden, Robert the Bruce, and the Bonnie Prince, and thousands of others dead on the moors of Scotland. It was no different here. Everyone wanted land, freedom, a chance at a decent life, and if that chance involved conquest, well, civilization had always been about conquest — the strong over the weak, intellect over instinct, and sometimes, though not always, good over evil.

Thunder rumbled to the south, and lightning danced, ghost-like, between the clouds. He shook his head to clear it of the past. In the present, they faced two real dangers, human and nature's, and both had to be reckoned with.

"What are you thinking?" Joanna's eyes were dark and serious under her wide hat brim.

"That we'd be better off in the hills than out here like a target."

She risked another glance around, saw only a veil of rain snaking up the valley, draining energy from its source, feeding feverishly on itself.

"Let's at least get out of this stream bed," she said. "It looks like a road, but it'll turn into a river when that storm hits."

He looked puzzled. "How?"

"This isn't Texas, but I'll bet it's the same. Run-off from rain's always tricky around here. Wait and see."

Her prediction was correct. Within an hour, what had been a dry route along the cañon floor was a wall of brown water, carrying brush, the branches of trees, anything unable to withstand its might. From where they'd stopped, in a narrow meadow that sloped upward, shielded by a canvas wrapped around them, Angus watched the fury — of storm, sky, running water — with awe.

"The Bible says . . . 'The meek shall inherit the earth,' " he said to Joanna, who huddled beside him under the canvas. "But there's nae a place for the meek in this land. They'd get swept away with the water."

"And what about Scotland?" she asked, aware of the heat of his body and her need to stay where she was.

"It's different, as I told you. But we're a tough lot. Still" — he squinted at the swirling clouds, gathered now in the crags overhead — "there's a similarity. Something that's almost like religion." He laughed self-consciously. "I'm not saying what I mean, lass. Pay me no mind."

But she'd felt it, too, and long before now. "It's like God lives in the earth," she said slowly. "In the middle of the storm. You said it just right. And He asks things we think are impossible, except, when we try, we grow a little bit, each time, until we're not who we thought we were at all." Then she laughed, too. "Listen to me, babbling like Clemmie."

"Nay, lass. You've just made sense of it. And here we are, hoping to get home with our hair in place. What do you feel about that?"

She shivered. "I don't know. Maybe we'll be lucky. I hope so. I'm not ready to die. Not yet."

"Nor I." There was so much he hadn't done, had wished to do. At the thought, he bent his head and kissed her. She tasted like the scented air, like growing things, fresh and green.

It had been so long since she'd been kissed or held. So long since she'd felt the stirrings of desire. Joanna closed her eyes and leaned into the strength of him, a whimper catching in her throat. She put her arms around him and drew him closer, glorying in his strength — and hers. Then, abruptly, she pushed him away and sat back, horrified at her own hunger.

"We mustn't!"

"It'd be a shame to die and not love each other, lass." His attempt at light-heartedness fell flat, as flat as he felt.

78

"Even so." She bowed her head, attempting to steady herself. It was the circumstances, she told herself, the danger, the electricity in the air. And to her eternal shame she hadn't thought of Alex once in at least two weeks, and here she was kissing someone almost a stranger and liking it too well.

"We won't do that again," she said, clasping her trembling hands in her lap.

Ah, but they would! He'd make sure of it — if they got out of here. He'd felt her answering warmth. It echoed in him still. Apaches or no Apaches, he'd see them home and lay his plans.

Without meeting her eyes, he said: "Don't be angry."

Surprisingly, she chuckled deep in her throat. "I'm not. But we can't afford to lose our wits." She threw off the canvas and looked around. The storm had moved on, the air was clear and sweet, and out in the valley, above it all, a rainbow deepened in color and arched, a banner of liquid light.

"See," she said, "there's our luck. And if we skirt the base of the mountain, we can get further away from here before dark."

Yes. There was still the night to be gotten through. A long one. He'd keep watch — retrieve his wits that had deserted him at the touch of her. Somehow, he'd get them home.

The desert night was dark, cold, filled with music. From somewhere came the trilling of what seemed like a thousand toads released from earthen burrows by the rain. Out on the plain, coyotes sang their hunting frenzy, and the air above was shattered by the constant calling of nighthawks.

In the wagon, Joanna slept. Angus sat with his back to it, rifle ready across his knees. How to tell which sounds were innocent and which were the stealthy Apaches with eyes that could see in the dark? He watched the mules, hoping their

79

senses were keen enough to warn him of what he might miss. And he watched the sky, saw meteors — more than he could have imagined — leaving vivid trails across the dark, some of them seeming so close he could hear them above all other sounds, a hiss, a crackle of dying fire.

We grow until we're not who we thought we were at all, Joanna had said. Wise woman! Out here, with only the hills and the stars to see, a man could become anything he wanted, good or bad, and no one to stop him. The magic had already taken hold of his senses. With Joanna beside him, the two of them could build an empire. If he could convince her. Damn Alex O'Keefe! His presence still haunted the place, still lived in her memory, a man who'd betrayed the woman he'd married, a woman too good to bear his name. He shook his head, knowing that she would, for sure, be along on the drive, that she was, in fact, a necessity, a balance wheel with her clear-eyed practicality coupled with her penchant for risk taking. And at trail's end, they'd all be other than who they were at the start. The journey would see to that — the danger, the unrelenting cruelty of the desert, the eye of the sun, following them westward to the sea.

Gradually the sky lightened, felt at first more than seen, a lifting, as if the cool wind was blowing away the dark. *Indians attack at dawn.* Somewhere he'd heard that. If so, now was the time.

Angus stood up slowly, stretched, looked around, seeing nothing unusual. In the wagon, Joanna stirred, opened her eyes, and saw the pale sky. "You were supposed to wake me!" She picked up her shotgun, climbed out, and stood beside him. "Why'd you let me sleep all night?"

"No reason to wake you. It's been quiet as a tomb. A good time for thinking."

"About what?"

"Everything. Hard to say. This country puts a mark on a person."

"Yes," she agreed, understanding immediately, "it does."

"Keep watch while I hitch the mules," he said, eyeing the shotgun. It was hardly a woman's weapon. "Are you sure you can handle that?" he asked, but was unprepared for the scornful look she gave him before she answered.

"I grew up with one. Where I lived, it was a good thing for a woman to be able to shoot. And believe me, I can."

He believed her. "That's good, then." One by one he led the mules to the stream to drink, then backed them on either side of the tongue, talking quietly as he did.

From where she stood, Joanna watched with approval. He had the touch with animals, firm but gentle. And yesterday he had kissed her, and she had responded. What on earth had possessed them? She'd never kissed any man but Alex, had never wanted to, and that had been right. Until now, with this man whose clear, blue eyes stabbed into her heart, read her mind, urged her on. But there were other demands on her, ones that needed a clear head, unmuddled by passion. This wasn't the time to react like an animal in season, if there ever was such a time.

"Let's leave as soon as you're done," she called over her shoulder, and then, scanning their back trail, saw a small knot of moving animals coming their way fast. "Something's moving out there. I'm not sure what."

"Should we stay or run?" he asked, then answered himself. "Best stay and fight right here. We'll not get a good aim out of a moving wagon." He unholstered his Irish Guards pistol, broke it open, checked the cartridges. "Between us, we'll give them something to remember, lass, and then some."

Together they watched, squinting against the rising glare of the sun that struck fire from rocks and sand, watched in silence and apprehension for long minutes that seemed like hours.

Six dark shapes and two riders materialized, and Joanna let out her breath. "It's our bulls!" she exclaimed. "The ones I bought from the Colonel."

He looked at her, then grinned. "And neglected to mention."

"I guess I forgot. I mean, I really did. So much else happened after that."

"Aye." Ah, she was a wonder, setting her own course and following without so much as a by your leave. "We'll meet them on the trail," he said. "Four of us might keep the Apaches away."

She was already climbing up on the seat. "And one of us will have a lot of explaining to do to John when we get in, I suppose."

"I'm leaving that task to you, lass. And I can hardly wait," he said, settling himself beside her and taking up the reins. "What's done is done, but, for sure, he'll have a lot to say. Count on it."

Chapter Eleven

They pulled into the ranch yard ahead of the bulls being driven by the cowboys. Joanna was exhausted but, knowing she'd have to face John's pessimistic reception, she braced herself.

John stood watching the cavalcade and was silent until the cowboys had corralled them, then turned to her, his face red. "Woman . . . ," he began.

"Shut up!" she said. "I know what you're going to say, and I don't want to hear it. I didn't spend money we can't afford. It was my own from the sale of my farm to spend as I chose. And I chose to get us some decent stock, instead of those . . . those skeletons you call cattle. Call it an early Christmas present." Then she turned and walked away.

Angus chuckled and slapped his brother on the shoulder. "Close your mouth, man. It's fly time as these Americans say. You might swallow one."

John spun on his heel and walked over to the corral, where he stood looking at the bulls. "She's crazed," he muttered. "Throwin' good money after bad, and us hanging on by our fingernails. And you hanging on her every word like she's some kind of miracle. First I had Alex and that girl, now you. When are you going to grow up?"

Angus had heard enough. He turned John around and hit him in the jaw, then looked down at him, where he had dropped. "Grow up yourself," he said. "If there's a fool around, it's not her. Nor me, either. And if you'd like some more of the same, get up and have at me. I'm bloody tired of your grousing."

83

John shook his head, felt his jaw, then amazed his brother by laughing. "I guess I deserved that," he said, getting up and feeling his jaw again. "I've not been myself lately." He crossed the yard, jumped on a horse that stood saddled, and took off at a high lope.

Joanna, who had been watching, came out. "You did that for me, didn't you?" she asked, looking up into Angus's eyes and remembering how his lips had felt, how prominent the bones of his face were under the skin.

"Aye," he said. "And for myself. He can be so pig-headed it makes a man lose his temper. But now he'll go and have a think for himself, and be back in time for supper."

She frowned. "Maybe I should have asked before I went off half-cocked."

He shook his head. "You said what you needed to . . . what he needed to hear. He's made a mess, but nothing so bad we can't fix it. He laid the groundwork, but now he needs help. That's where we come in." He grinned at Scotty who was tramping toward them. "And here's another we can count on, mark my words."

Scotty shuffled where he stood, embarrassed, but his eyes were bright. "I've been breakin' horses," he said to Joanna. "And there's one I'd like for you to take a look at."

"Another?" As always, the idea of horses distracted her.

"A nice little dun. You'll need more'n one on the trail."

She stifled a laugh. "How'd you know?"

"Ma'am, I knew. Reckon we all do. And when I saw you stick on that little bay the day the steer took after you, I said to myself, 'she's no lily-livered dude, for sure.' You want to take a look?"

"I do," she said. "Where is he?"

"I got him over here. Kept him special. He ain't big, but he's smart, and gentle. Runs like a jack rabbit." Scotty

84

pointed out the little buckskin. "If you want him, I'll break him easy."

Little ears pricked toward them. Large eyes watched, not out of fear, but curiosity. Joanna stopped, held out the back of her hand toward the black muzzle. "Hello, Poco," she said.

Beside her Scotty laughed. "That mean you like him?"

"I do. At least so far. Where's he from?"

He shrugged. "I'm not sure. He was runnin' with ours, but he ain't one of ours. No brand. My guess is he come acrost the line, found himself some company, and stayed. Could be he's already broke."

Joanna laid a careful hand on the muscled neck, noting that the horse made no effort to move away. "How many horses will we need for this drive?" she asked.

Scotty considered. "We oughta have at least six for every rider, but we don't. We'll have to make do with four."

"That many!"

"It's not nearly enough. We got to count on losses. And we'll need a wrangler for the remuda. The rest of us'll have our hands full just keepin' them cattle in line."

Suddenly she was in the position of having to find workers, and with no idea who to ask or how to go about it. "Who?" she asked. "Do you know anybody?"

He tugged his mustache. "Dunno. I'll ask around. Maybe Chapo's got a relative somewheres. Mexicans always got relatives."

"I'd be grateful." She smiled at the earnest little man. "I have a hunch I'll be saying that a lot. And thank you for finding me the little horse. He looks good to me."

Without meeting her eyes, he said: "Truth to tell, we're all grateful to you. We was wonderin' how long we'd have a job when you showed up. And him." He jerked his head toward Angus. "Meanin' no disrespect."

"None taken." On the contrary, his words gave her a feeling of satisfaction and confidence. The strength of any ranch lay in its riders as much as its owners, and that rôle had just been handed to her, woman or not. She said: "We'll do our best, Angus and I. I came here full of hope, and you know what I found. But I'm feeling hopeful again for different reasons, one of them being your trust in me. I'll try to live up to it."

She looked at the sky where a thunderhead pushed up behind the mountains, growing higher as she watched and more brilliant as it caught and reflected the rays of the sun. It seemed a visible sign, a portent of power drawn from the warm earth and the air. Unconsciously she flexed the muscles in her neck and shoulders, found them pliant, capable of bearing weight, and she stopped for a moment, feet planted firmly, and uttered a silent pledge. "I'll damn' well try."

Chapter Twelve

The tempo of life increased as the heat of summer faded. For the first time, with a goal firmly in place, everyone worked in unity, without complaint. Joanna had volunteered to help Scotty and Chapo with the green-broke horses, putting miles on those Scotty had judged were trustworthy. With her, always, were Chapo and his cousin, Juan Sextos, so named he said because he was the sixth in a line that went back beyond memory.

Juan Sextos had a way with horses. He spoke, and they listened, flicking their ears, obeying his smallest command. Juan Sextos was, Joanna decided, the answer to her prayer, and enchanted — half man, half horse. Not a horsebreaker like Scotty, but one with the creatures, with magic in his touch and the sound of his voice. She studied him as he breathed into the horses' flaring nostrils, calming the wildest of them with ease. Juan Sextos, she thought, was a marvel.

Terrill was rebuilding the old chuck wagon. Bought for a song, used on many previous roundups, it was rickety, and Tino had put his foot down. Unless it was fixed, they could go to the Pacific without him, an impossibility as they all knew.

Tino and Rain went to town with long lists of needed supplies — flour, salt, coffee, molasses, potatoes, canned tomatoes, extra water barrels that would be attached to the sides of the wagon, making it more unwieldy than it already was but necessary where they were going.

Angus and John poured over the rude map Deering had left them. It showed the route — almost a thousand miles of mostly desert, broken by the twisting of the Gila River, the location of known wells and water holes, and the Colorado River crossing. After that, the map was poorly marked, with only a twisting line to designate the trail and a few crosses marking known water holes.

Every time John allowed himself to think of what lay ahead, his stomach knotted. Would it all end out there somewhere, his dream, his chance, their bones scattered in a place they'd never seen? He kept his worries to himself, for, these days, Joanna and Angus had taken charge. That was another thing. The woman insisted on going along, and no one seemed inclined to stop her.

"Bad luck . . . a woman on the trail," Terrill grumbled. "But maybe she'll have a bellyful by the time we make Tucson."

"She's no quitter." Scotty came to her defense. "And she sits a horse as good as any of us."

"Then she can ride night duty," Terrill said with a grin. "Take some of the strain off."

"You best not let her hear you," Rain put in.

"And you'd best have some respect for your elders, kid. We all know you got a crush on her."

Rain blushed. "I don't!"

"It ain't no crime, and her a widow. If you play your cards right. . . ." Terrill stopped as John stepped between them.

"Get back to work. Rain, you have better things to do than stand here bickering. You, too, Terrill."

Just as John suspected, she was going to cause dissension, whether she meant to or not. He hoped Terrill was right, and she'd grow weary after a week or two, but, knowing her, he doubted it. He sighed, thinking that maybe he'd be the one to give up, stay in San Diego and run the business end. Sometimes he missed being in a city, missed the excitement, the noise, the restaurants, and worst of all he missed the Gaelic of his homeland.

Let Angus and Joanna stay and fight, take the risks. Hell, they both thrived on it all. And here she came over the rise, followed by the faithful Mexicans who thought she was some kind of saint. Still, she was doing a fine job with the horses. In spite of himself, he admired the way she was handling the big sorrel gelding, one of the last to be broken.

"How'd he go?"

She swung off. "Good. He won't give any trouble. And he's quick as a cat. Likes bossing cattle. I tried him on a few. He'll make a cutting horse with a little more work."

It was always a job, matching the horses to their work — cutting, night-herding, riding the roundup circle — and Joanna had found her place. She smoothed out the rough ones, put them all to the test out in the brush, then came back, sometimes with her face scratched, sometimes black and blue, and conferred with Scotty. Thanks to her, they were developing a fine string.

"There's few men could do a better job than you, lass," John said.

Praise? From him? Joanna stripped off her gloves and attempted to appear nonchalant. "I like doing it."

"Keep on, then." He walked away without noticing the sparkle in her eyes.

Angus had never been so tired in his life. After two weeks of roundup, all he wanted was a bed and a bath, in that order, and no chance of getting either one. He was discovering what every cattleman knew — that roundups were orderly chaos. They'd covered the southern end of the valley, bringing in unbranded calves and their mothers and all the two- and three-year-old steers that looked good enough to ship. Now they were working the mountains, the rocks, the narrow ledges where one slip meant injury or death to man and horse, and where the wily longhorns seemed to love to hide.

It had sounded easy enough in the beginning, like an adventure out of one of his children's books, but a few hours in the saddle had convinced him that his brother — and all the rest of them — were tougher men than an army of Scots. Dust, heat, flies, noise, unmanageable cattle, and days in the saddle that began before first light and ended, for a few hours, at dusk. Bone-jarring, dangerous labor, and all for a few dollars a head.

He'd seen Ellis Jackson, Deering's black foreman, have his horse gored by an enraged bull; Ellis barely escaped injury. He'd ridden the circle, gathering strays, and had them scatter like quail at the smallest excuse, which meant starting all over, on a tired horse, his own mouth so dry he couldn't spit. And once they were finished, they would have to hit the trail with the steers, a trail he'd memorized from the map and that seemed to stretch into infinity.

Still, there was something about the whole process that was close to happiness — the company of good men, the response of a fine horse, the sweetness of water after a long day, the sound of the night riders singing as they made their slow way around the steers. And there was always the sight of Joanna, her face brown, her long braid dust-caked, weary as the rest of them but holding her own with a grin and a flash of white teeth in spite of the fact that she was as tired as the rest of them.

Her acceptance by the men was gradual. They kept to themselves at first, excluding her from their rough camaraderie because they feared they'd do or say the wrong thing, rather than out of prejudice. She was, after all, one of the bosses and female, and there was no accounting for female ways. But she worked as hard as any of them, and it was

Terrill, thinking he'd show her up, who, instead, brought the respect of all of them to her.

"You ever cut a calf?" he'd asked, grinning that grin that grated on Joanna's nerves.

She was manning the gate of the rude corral as the newly branded and castrated calves were released and scrambled, bawling, for their mothers, a fierce group that stood watch on the other side bawling in answer.

She looked him straight in the eye. "Once or twice."

"Be a good thing for you to do here," he said. "Let the boys know the boss ain't no dude."

"I think they've figured that out already." She leaned and opened the gate to let a calf exit, at the same time using her horse to stem the mothers that pressed at the opening. "But if they need help, they know they can ask me."

"Scared?" He cocked a scraggly eyebrow.

"Not hardly." It was all she could do to keep her temper and her mind on the job.

He reined his horse over to the fire where the irons were heating. "Lady boss wants to try her hand."

"She can, if she wants." Ellis, born into slavery, didn't trust white men and this one in particular. His loyalty was to Deering who'd brought him, a free man, out of Georgia and into Arizona Territory where he'd proved his worth many times over. In Ellis's mind, Terrill Fox was no damn' good. The lady boss, well, she did what was needed and no whining. Look at her now, sitting on that big horse like she was born on him.

Her shout cut through the noise. "Terrill! Come, mind this gate!"

Still with that evil grin, he rode toward her. "They're waitin' on you. Hope you don't faint on us."

"Just watch me, cowboy!" Her answer hissed through

91

teeth gritted together. Would she never be finished proving herself?

She dismounted alongside Ellis. "Give me your knife," she said, her teeth still clenched. "Let's get it over with!"

Ellis smiled. She was mad clean through. He knew how she felt, having had to prove himself over and over. Bowing, he offered her the knife, handle first.

Scotty and Rain roped a calf, dragged him to the fire. Joanna knelt, cut, cut again, took the bleeding testicles and tossed them in the bucket, then stood and reached for the branding iron. Placing one foot on the calf's ribs, she left her mark — the **O MC**. And then she stayed, waiting for the next, and the one after that, never faltering, never losing control of the knife, the hot iron, the rhythm of it all, like a dance.

Oh, she was something to see! They all watched, even as they roped and dragged, and then hazed the finished calves toward the gate. The boss lady was a hand.

Ellis, off to one side, grew proud along with the rest. For sure, now they'd make their drive. For sure, with a woman like this as one of them — a woman who didn't quit — who'd called Terrill and shown him what for — who'd come out of nowhere like the rest of them, tossing that long braid of hers like any broomtail running fast and ahead of the rest and loving every minute of the long trail to freedom.

When she finished, Ellis offered his hand, and she took it, her eyes fierce, her grip firm.

He said: "You one heck of a lady, you don't mind me sayin' so."

Her teeth flashed white. "I don't mind. And you're one heck of a rep. I'll be pleased to have you with us."

He thought he'd serve her till doomsday, this white woman who gave as good as she got and never seemed to notice he was black as coal.

92

"We'll get these done, then take a breather," she said, eyeing the small bunch that was left.

From where he sat, Terrill sneered. Playing cowboy was what she was doing. Like that no-good husband of hers. Like that brother who thought he could come out here and run a ranch without knowing the first thing about the business or the country. He wished they'd all go back where they came from, wished he'd never laid eyes on them. Not even on Micaela. Especially not her — the whore.

His hands tightened on his reins, and his horse, sensitive to pressure, side-stepped, letting the gate swing open. Within seconds, three cows were in the corral headed for their calves, heedless of whatever stood in their way. One of them spotted Joanna kneeling on the ground, and, without hesitating, charged.

"Look out!" Scotty, holding the rope around the calf's heels, shouted, then let loose and rode between Joanna and the maddened mother, his quick thinking giving her a second to scramble to her feet and swing up behind Ellis on his horse.

"Hang on tight," Ellis growled.

"Don't worry."

Someone got a rope around the maddened cow's horns, and Scotty caught her by one heel and held her there, bellowing and blowing slobber.

"Dammit, Terrill! You watchin' that gate or ain't you?" he yelled at Terrill, sickened at the thought of what might have happened.

"It was an accident. The damn' horse spooked."

"Then get one you can handle!"

The cows were dragged out, and Joanna, knees shaking, slid to the ground. "That was close," she said to Ellis. "Thanks. You, too, Scotty. I owe you. Now let's get back to work."

No one argued with the set of her jaw, or failed to notice that she ignored Terrill as if he weren't there, as if he hadn't almost caused her injury if not death. Inside, she was furious. Terrill was a thorn in her side, but there wasn't much she could do about it now, when they needed every hand. But someday it would give her the greatest pleasure to tell him off and be rid of him.

"Think it was an accident?" Ellis asked Scotty a few minutes later.

"Maybe."

"That Terrill, he mean as two buckets of snake shit."

In spite of himself, Scotty laughed. "You got that right. I'll keep an eye on him."

"Me, too."

The two men loped back to the fire, preoccupied. Joanna had proven herself. Boss lady or not, she was one of them now.

Chapter Thirteen

The buzzards had flown south. Nights were cold, and there was a skim of ice on water tanks and under the creek banks in the early mornings. Overhead, the sky arched, a cloudless, nearly transparent blue.

They headed out at first light on the 5th of December, driving twelve hundred steers and a *remuda* of seventy horses. Tino and the lumbering chuck wagon left first, his destination that night's camp at Apache Wells, twenty miles north.

Joanna, riding her sturdy little bay, watched until Tino was only a moving speck amidst the grass and dried yucca stalks that dotted the valley. She shivered as the herd, led by Ellis Jackson and Deering's old lead steer, Rupert, began to move. The ground shook, the silence was shattered by the sound of thousands of hoofs striking rocks and earth, and she felt the uneasiness of the bawling animals being driven into the unknown. *So are we all,* she thought and smiled at Angus, who sat beside her.

He returned the smile, his eyes a deep and serious blue. "Take a good look. Here's that history we talked about in the making."

She closed her eyes. "It's scary. All of a sudden, it's scary. Talk's so easy, and then it starts to happen. Just a couple months ago, this was a dream around a dinner table."

"If it wasn't for dreamers, the world wouldn't be as it is," he said.

"How so?"

"Someone dreamed ships once. And sails. Someone

dreamed new worlds and how it would feel to live in them . . . how it would be to be free. John had a dream. So did you." He purposely avoided mentioning Alex.

But she remembered, and her laugh was bitter. "And it turned into a nightmare."

"But look now. You've turned it 'round, and here we are setting off on an adventure. A lucrative one, too."

"I hope we're doing the right thing."

He settled his hat firmly. "Right, wrong, we have to do something. We're in the middle, lass, and now we'll have to learn to swim. And since we're supposed to be riding with Juan and the *remuda,* let's catch up, or we'll miss it all."

Juan greeted them with a grin. "A fine day, *señora,*" he called. "May God go with us."

"I hope so, Juan." In spite of her fears, she looked over the horses with an approving eye, picking out her favorites. Would all of them make it to California, or would some drop by the way, injured, exhausted, left to live or die on their own?

She shook her head to drive away her demons. As Juan had said, it was a fine day, a good omen. Abruptly she pulled off to the side of the horse herd and kept pace just behind the leaders. Deering had advised that she not interfere with the boys who were pushing the cattle until they were used to the trail, and just as well. She was happiest here, watching the tossing manes, the curious eyes, with a wind at her back and the valley opening up as they moved north. To the west, the mountains began to gleam like rubies as the rising sun caught them, tinted them, seemed to create them anew out of the flesh of the rock.

For a few miles John rode beside Rain who'd been forced into drag position at the rear of the herd. He felt for the kid, the youngest of them all, but as good as the best in his opin-

96

ion. Back here they choked on the fine dust that stung their eyes and gritted between their teeth, but Rain seemed cheerful enough.

"My ma always said we got to eat a peck of dirt before we die," he shouted. "Reckon I'll have done that before we get where we're going."

"And then some," John agreed, his words muffled by the bandanna he'd pulled over his face. He wasn't sure of the protocol of trail driving, but it seemed cruel to doom the kid to this spot for a thousand miles. Terrill's doing, of course. "You get the drag, kid," he'd announced that morning, and, without waiting for an argument, had spurred off. Terrill took too much for granted, John thought. He'd have a talk with Deering, when they camped for the night. After all, Terrill wasn't running the show, although he acted like he was.

A steer broke away, followed by another, both determined to go back where they'd come from.

"I'll get 'em!" Rain wheeled around, and John's big sorrel jumped to block a third, reaching out and biting the startled animal on its rump.

Rain was having trouble. The steers were going in opposite directions. As soon as he headed one and turned him, it would take off again, aiming for the hills. Damned critters! And this was nothing compared to what a thousand of them could do.

Deering came at a lope out of nowhere. Together, he and Rain rounded up the recalcitrant steers and pushed them back into the bunch.

"Could've been worse." Deering wiped his face with his sleeve, smearing the dust that caked his eyebrows.

"And probably will be," John stated.

"Cheer up, friend. Think about the money."

John had. Why else agree to this torture? And he was still of a mind to stay in California, give the place over to Angus and Joanna, receive his checks, and never look at a cow again. Anyone with half an eye could tell his brother was besotted with the woman, and good luck to him. A driving female she was to be sure. He tried to spit and found his mouth gone dry.

Deering laughed. "Try a chew. Or a pebble. Keeps the wet in your mouth."

"I'd as soon swallow a stone as tobacco juice." John's pipe was in his jacket pocket. He wished it was between his teeth, but pleasure had no place in this endeavor, none at all that he could see. Pleasure came later with a little money to spend on himself for a change, and, perhaps, even on a woman. A soft one, smelling of soap and perfume, her hair in ringlets, as unlike Joanna as possible.

His daydream was cut short as half a dozen longhorns broke loose, and the sorrel turned on his foreleg and took off after them. Good money on the hoof, headed for the high pastures. John settled himself in the saddle and let the horse go. Deering was off to one side, his face set, no doubt thinking the same thing — three hundred dollars scattered to the wind.

Scotty came up beside him. "I'll turn 'em!" he shouted. His horse was small and fast, and he passed John and Deering easily, then caught up to the two slowest steers and began moving them in a half circle. Before he could complete his plan, his horse stumbled and went down head first, hind legs thrashing in a cloud of dust. Scotty landed ahead of it and lay still.

John reached him first, relieved to see the little man sitting up. "Are you hurt?"

One side of Scotty's face was scraped raw, but he shook his head. "Got the wind knocked out of me. Maybe bunged up

98

my shoulder, but it ain't broke." His expression changed as he saw his horse, one leg dangling. "God damn." He limped over and put a hand on the animal's shoulder. "His leg's broke." He risked a look at John, misery written all over his face. "I'm sure sorry, boss."

John swallowed hard. "Best shoot him and be done with it."

"Get me another horse, and I'll wait till the herd's out of earshot. Havin' them take off is all we need."

John rode after the *remuda,* his shoulders slumped. This was what happened. You killed off your horses, injured your men, all for a bunch of damned cattle. And he'd come here with such expectations, so sure that all he'd have to do was supply enough grass. The taste in his mouth was bitter. He took out his pipe and wedged it between his teeth, noting that it gave cold comfort.

Juan came to meet him, brows raised in a question. *"¿Señor?"*

"Rope me a horse. Scotty's broke a leg." It hurt to say it.

"¡Por Dios!" Juan shook out his rope. It had been a good horse. One of the best. But these things happened. Horses died. And men. It was the way of things, the will of God. Juan was glad he was not God and so spared the decision about who was to die and when.

"What happened?" Joanna rode up, her instinct telling her something was very wrong.

John told her.

"Let me take it." She held out her hand for the rope. "You go on back with the herd. Sounds like they need all the help they can get."

She found Scotty sitting on a rock, his saddle beside him. "Figured you'd come," he said, getting to his feet.

"How'd it happen?"

He sighed. "Dunno. Maybe he caught a foot in the rocks. Maybe just slipped. You go on. I'll catch up."

She looked at the gray horse standing on three legs, its head drooping. "He was a goer."

Scotty blinked. "Yeah. Now git. They say it gets easier, but it don't."

She heard the shot from a half mile away. Scotty was right. Death never came easily. Not here.

The moon was rising — a half moon — but it filled the valley with light, turned the world into black shadows and startling silver surfaces. Joanna, unable to sleep, stood at the entry of her tent and looked out at the resting cattle, a solid mass except for the light that glinted off their horns. One of the night riders was singing, the words unintelligible, the melody soothing. Probably Chapo, she thought, crooning one of the Mexican songs that seemed to flow from him like honey — sweet and somehow mournful like the land itself.

"Can't sleep?" Deering came around the corner, his cigar glowing in the darkness.

"No. And I'm exhausted." Exhausted couldn't explain how she felt, bone weary, saddened by the loss of the horse, but with a humming deep inside as if she were still moving, still a part of an unstoppable flood.

"Best sleep while you can," he advised. "There'll be nights when you wish you could."

"You've done this before?"

"Not on such a scale, but it's not that different. Cattle are herd animals. One brain among them all, or so it seems. The only sure thing is that brain will kick in when you least expect it, and then you've got trouble. Plenty of it."

"Will we make it?" She spoke what had been eating at her since morning.

He puffed his cigar before answering. "With luck. It's a gamble, but so's life. You can play it safe, or go out and make things happen." He chuckled. "And you're the second kind, you know. You've got us all going. Seems as if we were bogged down in our own problems till you came along. Look at John."

"I did," she said, then laughed with him. "He's had a hard time."

"Nothing worth getting comes without a fight."

"It seems that's all I've been doing since I got off the train."

"Don't quit till we get where we're going. Having a lady boss keeps us all on our toes."

She shivered. The night was cold, the kind of cold that got under the skin. "I'm not stopping there, either," she said, thinking of her plans.

"I didn't guess you would. You buying more land? More stock?"

Her smile was enigmatic. "Certainly."

Whatever her ideas, she was keeping them to herself, and he'd watch with interest. He tossed his cigar on the ground and mashed it with his boot heel. "Best get to sleep. Plenty of time to talk in San Diego."

Inside again, she took off her jacket and boots. No sense undressing further, down to the long johns she wore beneath her skirt. Besides, the cold penetrated even through the tent walls, rose up out of the ground. With a sigh she crawled under the blankets, wishing Angus was with her, his body warm and comforting. She wasn't made to sleep alone, to lie forlorn and empty, making her own warmth and finding no solace in it.

Stifling a sob, she curled up, wrapped her arms around herself, and shortly slept.

Chapter Fourteen

"Hey! Six Toes! Catch me my horse, too!" Terrill's voice cut through the chill air, startling Juan Sextos who was leading Joanna's buckskin. The skinny *gringo* seemed to delight in making fun of his name, in treating him as if he were an ignorant slave, instead of a man in charge of horses. At first he had laughed. Now he was insulted, and by this man who was no better than he. Juan opened his mouth to answer, but the right English words wouldn't come, only the Spanish — plenty of them — which he was sure the *gringo* wouldn't understand.

"Don't stand there with your mouth open. You heard me."

"We all heard you." John stepped away from the chuck wagon where he'd been finishing a cup of coffee, Joanna and Angus beside him. "And you know full well that each of you catches your own horse."

"I was joking." Terrill was unfazed at being caught. "A man's got to have some fun."

"Not at the expense of somebody else. And it's about time you learned how to pronounce Juan's name," Joanna put in.

"Like I said, it was in fun."

John nodded once curtly. "Aye. And enough of it. Catch up the horse. And ride drag today."

Terrill stiffened. "That's Rain's job."

"It's every man's job. We rotate. You know it, as well as I do."

He wanted to tell them all to go to hell, especially her with that damned superior look on her face. She'd change her tune soon enough, if she knew the truth, wouldn't she just? But the time to tell her wasn't now with her two partners hanging around. He'd choose his time, and wipe that snotty look right off her face. Abruptly he picked up his rope and left them without apology.

Angus looked after him. "He's a born troublemaker."

John peered into his cup as if he could read the future in its contents. "Good hands are hard to come by. He'll have to do till we can find a better one."

Joanna said: "Do we need him at all? He's like a rotten apple."

"We'd be askin' for it to fire him now, lass . . . us out here, and him with vengeance in his head. Just let him be, and keep your distance if you can."

She swung up on the buckskin. "Believe me, I'll do that. I can't stand him. Angus, are you riding with me?"

"I am." He intended to stick to her like a burr, and, if trouble came, he'd get her out or die trying. Except he had no intention of dying, not until they were both old and could look back and laugh.

"We'll stop tonight at the *cienega*," John said. "There's old pens there for the horses. Tell Juan to put the night horses in."

Angus frowned. "*Cienega?* What's that?"

"Kind of a water hole. The river comes up from underground, and there's trees and good grass. Rustlers used the place. Probably still do. That's why the pens. If we're lucky, we'll have it to ourselves."

"And if we're not?"

"There's enough of us to make a difference."

The river surfaced beside a bluff, running above ground for half a mile before disappearing again, its channel marked by a twisting wash studded with cottonwoods.

Two men scrambled to their feet as the chuck wagon came toward them.

"What in hell's that?" asked one.

"Looks like dinner," was the other's response.

Behind Tino, the dust of the oncoming herd spiraled skyward. The first man glanced back at the corral where eight horses stood watching. "Hope none of these belong to whoever that is." He pointed in the direction of the dust cloud.

"They ain't branded. We found 'em. Hell, nobody knows who we are. We're just out here looking for work."

Upon seeing the strangers, Tino's first impulse was to turn back and give warning. But there were only two men, and he was armed, although he'd had little chance to practice with the .45. Besides, the front riders weren't far behind. Somewhat cautiously, he crawled down off the seat.

"Howdy." Tino liked the sound of that word — had ever since he'd first heard it. So American. So he used it every chance he got.

"Howdy, yourself." The taller of the two stood staring at him as if thinking over possibilities.

Tino pretended not to notice, unharnessing the mules and leading them to water, the man at his heels. "I am called Tino," he said.

"You Messican?"

He drew himself up. "I am from Italia."

The man began rolling a cigarette. "Where's that at?"

Imagine! Imagine not knowing such a simple thing! But then, in this place, so many people were ignorant, right down to making marks on paper to sign their own names. He thought a minute, searching for words this man would understand.

Finally he gestured toward the east. "Far," he said. "Across the ocean."

The man licked the cigarette paper, stuck the end in his mouth, and spoke around it. "You *seen* the ocean?"

"I came here on it."

"What's it like?"

Tino thought again. "Very big. From one side you can't see the other."

"I'll be damned." The man blew a cloud of smoke.

Tino agreed, but didn't answer, and, after hobbling the mules, he turned back to the wagon. Remembering the rules of frontier hospitality, he said: "You can eat with us."

The man stared down the valley. "A big outfit."

"Yes."

"Big as that ocean of yours?"

Tino smiled. "They would all drown in that ocean, and you wouldn't find them."

"Where you headed?"

So many questions! *One more,* Tino decided, *I'll answer one more.* "California."

The man sneered. Turning, he called to his friend. "Hey, Will. Tino, here, says they're drivin' to California!"

Will grinned, showing a lack of upper teeth. "Shit!"

"This is funny?" Tino asked.

"It won't be when them cattle are dying of thirst. I was fixin' to ask for a job, but no thanks. What outfit you with anyhow?"

Tino drew himself up. "This is the Artesia and the Circle MC. And you haven't said how you are called."

"Just don't call me late to supper." The man laughed and slapped his knee, then frowned. "That's a joke. You ain't laughing."

Something in his eyes made Tino wish he was some place

105

else. He smiled. "Me, I don't always understand these American jokes."

"That's right. You're one of them furriners. Where from again?"

Tino was saved from having to answer when the *remuda* came into sight. He sighed with relief. Everywhere in this place were men who made their living with guns, and these two were obviously that kind. Now at least he would have reinforcements, if this ignorant person took offense.

"Hey! Damn! That's a woman!" Will exclaimed, gesturing to his buddy.

Joanna was in the lead, and there was no mistaking her sex, even bundled into her thick jacket. "She is one of the bosses, *signore,*" Tino said.

"Does she put out?"

He looked at his questioner with suspicion, not sure of his meaning. "I think, *signore,* you had better watch what you say. She is fine lady. Very fine."

"Too good for the likes of me, you mean."

Tino chose not to answer at all. He walked to the rear of the wagon, took a shovel, and began to dig a pit for his fire. The sooner these two were fed and sent on their way, the better he was going to feel.

If Mellen Deering hated anything worse than a Yankee or an Apache, it was a horse thief. In the past, he'd spent weeks chasing stolen horses, and he'd never come back without them. More than one cañon in the mountains hid the bones of those foolish enough to appropriate his property or that of his neighbors. The punishment for horse stealing was hanging. Lacking judge, jury, or a rope, a lead slug did as well, or better. Rough justice, but justice, nonetheless, in Deering's mind and in the minds of anyone who knew the situation.

106

He spotted the sleek red dun horse among the eight in the pen as soon as he rode into camp and recognized it as one of Harrington's. "Well, well," he said to Tino, "we have company."

"And no good, I think." Tino looked over his shoulder to make sure they hadn't heard.

"I think you're right." Mellen walked closer to take a better look. The horse wasn't branded, but there was no mistaking him or where he'd come from. "Well, well," he said again. "Caught you."

Angus didn't like the way the strangers' eyes lingered on Joanna. They hadn't the right to watch her that way, like a pair of coyotes circling their prey. He wanted to knock their heads together. He wanted them gone.

"Who do they think they are?" he muttered to Deering.

"Leave them to me."

The older man's eyes were unreadable, cold as gray ice. Angus recognized a killer when he saw one, and Deering, regardless of his usual jovial attitude, was that. "Have a care man," he said.

Deering laughed once, like a fox. "I always do."

A hard wind kicked up out of the north. The herd was restless, wanting to turn south, away from the bitter gusts.

"Won't take much to set 'em off tonight," Ellis observed, putting his plate in the wash barrel and sniffing the air. "It'll maybe snow soon, too."

Joanna moved closer to the fire. "Does it snow hard here?"

"I seen it ten foot deep in the mountains, maybe more some years. Down here it's not that bad. Usually melts in a day." Tonight it was the wind that had him and the rest of the men worried. One skittering tumbleweed would set the steers off. "Don't sleep too sound, ma'am," he advised her. "Once they get going, they run right over the top of whatever's in front of 'em." He was dead serious.

"After that, I probably won't sleep at all."

"And I'm sleeping outside your door, lass." Angus walked back from the wash barrel. "Our company leaves a lot to be desired."

She'd noticed the two men and their hungry glances, but the idea of Angus posting himself as watchdog was ridiculous. "I have this." She patted her .45. "I'll be all right."

"You will, and that's a fact," he said, unswerved from his purpose.

It was cold. If she invited him in, out of the wind, what then? The loneliness of the night before still haunted her. The touch of his lips was a vivid presence. It would be easy, so easy, to open her arms and bring him in, chasing away ghosts, warming herself at his fire. *Selfish reasons,* she thought. And love, to her, was giving, not taking.

"I'll be fine," she said again. "But thank you."

He didn't want her thanks. He wanted. . . . Abruptly he got to his feet. Never mind what he wanted. There was danger all around — in the air, in the cunning of men, the instincts of animals. His wants would have to wait.

"I'm doubling the riders," Ellis said. "Better safe than sorry."

Angus wanted to volunteer — he wanted to go — he wanted to stay close to Joanna. "If you need me . . . ," he began.

Ellis shook his head. "I'd be happier if you stayed here. You ain't never been in a stampede. You will be before this trip's over, and it ain't no picnic. But, tonight, you got something else to do." Besides, he had no intention of nursemaiding the uninitiated through a mess of cattle.

Chapter Fifteen

Like the flexing of one long, smooth muscle, the herd took off at moonrise. The only good thing, Ellis said later, was that there was enough light to see by. From her tent Joanna felt the ground vibrate, heard the pounding hoofs, and leaped to her feet. Outside the noise was worse, trapped by the mountains and echoing back, wave after wave, a constant, buffeting thunder.

She held to Angus's arm and watched, too stunned by what she saw to be frightened yet — the mindless rush of mottled bodies, clashing horns, and, beside and behind them, the riders going flat out, attempting what seemed impossible — the control of a vast and living thing that had no sense or ability to reason, that existed only for flight.

Chapo, with Rain behind him, caught up with the front runners. It was like trying to wrestle a mess of giant snakes, Rain thought. One mis-step and you were finished, pounded into ground meat, not enough left to bury. "Oh, Jesus," he moaned, then clamped his jaws shut and rode, keeping abreast, edging closer, pushing, pushing, trying to slow the damned critters, change their direction, trusting his horse to stay on its feet and out of the way of hoofs and slashing horns.

A cloud blotted out the moon, leaving only a faint light, but the wind was on Rain's cheek now, instead of at his back. They had to be circling, unless the wind had changed. Ahead, the mountains were black, darker than the sky. His horse jumped a low-growing bush, dodged a lethal horn, and he hung on, cursing. But somehow they'd managed, he and

Chapo, to turn the slobbering bastards. Across the tossing backs, across at least a mile of valley, he saw Ellis riding his white night horse, acting like the axle of a huge wheel, and behind him, a shadow rider, probably Terrill, letting them swing and surround him on both sides. A bad place to be, he decided, then cursed again as his tired horse stumbled, then caught itself. He grabbed for the horn. That's what the thing was there for. A handle when you needed it most, a slight edge between a man and dying.

The herd slowed to a trot. In spite of the wind and the cold, Rain was soaked with sweat, caked with dust and slobber. And it would be hours before he could wash his face in icy water, grab a cup of Tino's strong coffee, and take the chill away.

"*¡Bueno, amigo!*" Chapo called back to him. "*¡Bueno!*"

After all, there were compensations. He was alive. He'd won the praise of a seasoned rider. His discomfort evaporated as quickly as it had come. He'd done it. For sure, this night, he'd won his spurs.

At the first sound of hoofs, John McLeod and Deering were mounted and running.

"Ellis said for us to stay back. When they turn . . . if they turn . . . we ride swing."

If they turned. For all John knew, they could be back where they'd started by morning, and Ellis's orders gone up in smoke. It had all come to this — chaos in the night, lunacy, the noise like one of the circles of hell, and himself sucked among the charging beasts against his will. He was riding as he'd never had to ride, becoming a part of the horse, and thank God for the moon, the agility of the creature under him, the intelligence that made him man, able to think ahead, to survive and function.

Slowly — so slowly he wasn't sure of it at first — the pace lessened, the mass swung to the left, reluctantly, to be sure, but tired now, the memory of panic vanished in the dust. He and the riders had become the brain. They were the controllers of a thousand destinies. "By Christ," he said to himself, pushing against the moving flank, and rode on.

The herd was bunched, run-out, but not bedded down. Some final resistance lingered in each body, moved each head, caused them to bawl at one another before quieting.

"No more fight in the buggers tonight. Just noise," Ellis commented, when he rode up to John, his dark face sweat-streaked, his teeth white in the moonlight.

"And a good thing." Even years in the saddle hadn't prepared John for the stress of the stampede. His body ached in every joint as if it had been twisted, wrung out.

"Me and the boys'll handle them now." Ellis knew just how he felt. He'd been the same way the first time he'd chased after a bunch of locoed steers in the dark. "You OK, boss?" he asked as Deering joined them.

"Right as rain."

"You two want to go on back?" Ellis hesitantly suggested by way of a question. "I reckon Miz O'Keefe'll want to know what happened."

Spoken like a man who knew precisely who he was, John thought with admiration. "You did good work," he said.

"I'm paid for it. I had help." Ellis wheeled and trotted off.

As the two men approached camp, Deering looked around. "Well, well," he said, "it seems our birds have flown."

"Good riddance." The saddle tramps were the last thing on John's mind. It was coffee and the fire that lured him.

"And we're probably shy a few horses."

John straightened at that. "Are you sure?"

"I will be, once I take a look."

A man's property wasn't safe anywhere in this country. John muttered a curse.

"Don't worry. I'll handle it," Deering assured.

John knew how his neighbor operated. Still, the idea of him going off on his own worried him. "Are you sure, man?" he asked again.

"I'm sure." There was a cold conviction in Deering's voice. "Just give me a couple days."

"You want us to wait?"

He shook his head. "Time is money. You all go ahead. I'll catch up."

With mixed feelings, Angus watched his brother ride toward them. Here he was, young, able, the equal of any man in a fist fight or with pistols, yet forced to stay behind when clearly all hands had been needed.

As if she read his mind, Joanna said: "I hope I never see anything like that again."

"You will, lass. It's the nature of the beasts, so it seems."

"I should've been with them."

"Aye. And gotten yourself killed. Best leave it to those who know what they're about."

She stepped away from him, eyes glittering. "And I don't?"

"That's not what I meant, and you know it. I'm the one who should've been out there."

"But stayed because you think I need a guardian." Her voice was bitter. "Because I can't be trusted to take care of myself."

He understood her anger. It was the same as his own. "Nay, lass," he said softly. "It's because you're the brains of

112

the outfit. We cannot spare you. You're our luck, don't you see?"

Oh, he could talk his way out of a maze with that soothing voice, that lilting burr that got under her skin! How many women had fallen for him, warmed to him, lusted after him?

"Flatterer!" she snapped, hoping he'd not notice the effect of his words.

"It's the truth, and you're too hard-headed to see it." He broke off as John dismounted stiffly. "Are you all right, man?"

"I'll live. I think. We got most of them. The boys will look for strays in the morning. A nasty business." He could still feel it, see it, that monstrous wave of animals running amok, sweeping him along as if he were a leaf, as if he counted for nothing at all. And there stood his brother and the woman, unruffled, untouched, as if it were all a game to be applauded from the sidelines. "We could've used your help," he blurted suddenly, unable to control his anger.

Angus stifled the hot words that came to mind. It wasn't the time or the place. "You'll have it from now on. There's not a McLeod born who's a coward."

"I didn't mean. . . ."

"I know what you meant. I'm just clearing the air."

"And I'm going to bed," Joanna said. If they were going to fight, they could do it without her. "Thank you both."

From inside her tent, she heard their voices, low but tinged with irritation. At times like this, she wished she were a man, with a man's strength. She wished she understood herself and what she was doing out here, risking not only her life, but the life of all those with her. And just before she fell asleep, she wished she'd never laid eyes on Alexander O'Keefe or relied on his dreams of grandeur.

Chapter Sixteen

Mellen Deering hummed to himself as he tightened the cinch on the blaze-faced bay, the horse he'd never been able to tire out, no matter what. Some time between the stampede and the first gray light of morning, a light snow had fallen, glossing the ground, shimmering on the branches of the mesquites, the pointed yucca leaves. Pretty. And helpful. Tracks showed plain in the whiteness. Hoofs sank deeply in the damp left by the melting snow. Two men. Now with twelve horses, four of them the property of his own outfit. And no way for them to hide. Still humming a tune that might have been that old Confederate song of battle, "The Bonnie Blue Flag," Deering rode out quietly, headed back toward Apache Wells.

He took his time, being a patient tracker. After a few hours, he left the trail for one closer to the mountains, one that gave more cover. They wouldn't be watching for anyone there, if they watched at all. He rode on humming, stopped at noon for a lunch of cold biscuits and water. The horse was still fresh, even eager, pointing its ears southward.

"Easy," he told it. "Easy."

Outside Joanna's tent, Angus slept fitfully. It was cold, and his mind kept churning. What he wanted to do was to lift the tent flap and go in to her, take her in his arms, savor the lovely sweet warmth of her body against his own. But then he saw Deering.

Without being told, he knew the reason for Deering's stealthy departure. So, after a few minutes, he climbed out of

114

his bedroll and stood listening to the faint music of the night riders and the sound of hoofs moving steadily toward the south. "I think I'll just go along and even the odds," he said to himself, his breath making a cloud in the chill air. He walked to the chuck wagon where the coffee pot stood on the fire and poured himself a cup.

"Tell my brother I've gone with Deering," he said to Tino who looked up from his Dutch oven.

Tino nodded. "Be careful, *signore*. Those are ver' bad men."

"That's why I'm going."

Tino put the last of the biscuits into the oven and placed the lid on top. "Better there are two of you," he said.

The coffee had warmed Angus. He swung onto his horse and headed out at a careful walk. It was an easy trail to follow. He kept his distance behind Deering, found where he'd cut off toward the mountains, and did the same. Two against two — or maybe not. He had the strong feeling there were more of the thieves than that, and he'd learned to trust his instinct.

The two men had made camp at nightfall, using the old adobe wall of an abandoned house as protection from the wind. Deering saw the light of their fire, the stolen horses bunched at the edge of the tank where the tules were frost-etched, the grass trampled. He left his bay tied securely to a juniper and circled around so the fire would be in their faces, while he remained in darkness. The night was bitter. The air tasted of more snow to come.

He had killed his first man, a Yankee soldier, at sixteen, and he had learned that all it took was resolution. At eighteen, the war over, he had returned home and found nothing but boards and ashes and the graves of his parents under the grape arbor. Ellis Jackson was the one person left who had seen what had happened, although Mellen had had to pry the story out of him. Rape, pillage, murder — he'd seen it, lived through it, but somehow had never believed it would happen to his own. He had left for Arizona the next day, accompanied by the loyal Ellis, and he'd never looked back. Nor had he ever forgotten what he'd learned, the hatred that rose in him at the sight of his youth wiped out in one brief hour.

"Wish we could've got a piece of that filly." Will gave his toothless grin.

His partner laughed. "Like the furriner said . . . 'she's a lady.' Besides, what'd she want with you?"

"They're all the same lyin' down."

"I never heard of no woman on the trail before."

"Me, neither. Reckon she's just along for some fun with the boys . . . never mind, he said, 'she's a lady.' I bet she's a real piece."

It had gone far enough. Deering stepped out into the circle of firelight. "Shut up!" he commanded. "And don't move."

They froze like rabbits, and he smiled without humor. Maybe he'd let them beg. Maybe he'd run down the list of their crimes, not the least of which was their talk about Joanna.

"You've got horses that belong to me," he said. "And you've got no call to talk about a lady like that. I guess you know what the penalty for horse stealing is." His eyes shifted from his pistol to just over his shoulder. He heard the crackle of dry brush just before two shots ripped through the dark, and he hit the ground, rolling.

"Stop right where you are!" a man called out.

There was no mistaking the voice or the man stepping out of the dark. "What the hell are you doing here?" Deering demanded as he pushed himself up quickly.

Angus kept his pistol trained on the two who'd frozen again in the act of scrambling for their guns. "I decided to help even the odds, man. There was another, creeping up behind you."

Deering stood up. "I owe you."

"We're all in this together," Angus said. "What about these two?"

"I'll take care of them." Deering fired twice, watched expressionlessly as the two men staggered and fell. Then he said: "Where's the other one?"

Angus took a moment to answer. He'd known killers, but none as relentless as this man. "Dead. At least, I think he is."

"Why'd you come after me?" Deering replaced his pistol in its holster. He was curious about this McLeod brother, so different from John.

"A gut feeling. I've learned to listen to it."

"And a damn' good thing for me you did. Let's get those horses and move out."

Angus looked at the bodies, the blood pooling on the sand. "What about them?"

"Leave 'em. If they have more friends, maybe it'll be a lesson. Take their guns and saddles. Probably that's all they have that's worth a damn."

Out on the flat a coyote barked and was answered by another and another. Already the scavengers were gathering, attracted by the scent of death.

Deering scattered the ashes of the fire, then roped the horses, head to tail. It was easier traveling that way. Then he mounted the bay and sat looking at the bodies for a long while. Christ it was cold! And he hadn't slept for two nights. Time for that when they'd caught up with the rest.

"Let's get on back," he said.

Chapter Seventeen

"Where is *Señor* Angus?" Joanna took the reins of her horse from Juan who shrugged in answer and turned away without meeting her eyes.

She mounted and looked around, saw the usual frenzy of breaking camp — riders, horses, cattle churning the snow into mud, Tino already on the seat of the chuck wagon. But no Angus. Funny how without him the whole scene seemed flat, a one-dimensional picture postcard lacking warmth or intimacy. Funny how she felt inside — hollow, as if she were a stranger. Spotting John and Ellis, she trotted over to them.

"Where's Angus?" Her voice rose above the confusion.

John, well aware of Deering's vigilante activities, pulled on his hat brim and thought before he answered. "He and Mellen went after some stray horses."

"Strays?" Her forehead puckered. They couldn't afford to lose horses. "How many?"

"Maybe half a dozen."

Ellis said: "Not to worry, ma'am. Mister Deering, he knows what he's doing."

She supposed she could believe them. Still, it was odd that Angus hadn't said anything, and odder still that she felt like the wind had been knocked out of her. "That's all right, then," she said, and wondered if it was.

"And, ma'am?" Ellis, reading her thoughts, decided to take her mind off them. "Ma'am, remember, we got to get those cattle through the pass and as far away from those railroad tracks as we can before the afternoon train comes through. I'm countin' on you and Juan to handle the hosses. Get them out ahead."

There had been some talk the night before about the train, but she hadn't really listened. Now she asked: "What happens if we don't?"

His face was grim. "Ain't no such thing as don't. These cattle never seen a train in their lives. One look at that engine, one sound out of that whistle, and that trouble last night'll seem like play time."

"I see." And in her mind she did. Steers dying on the tracks, the rest scattered from hell to breakfast. She straightened up. "I'll do my best."

"I'm countin' on it." He tipped his hat and rode toward the herd.

The *playa* was snow-covered, its whiteness made more brilliant by the reflection of the sun off the shallow pools of water where thousands of birds spent the winter. A group of cranes took flight ahead of the *remuda,* and the air was filled with the beating of wings and their mournful calling. They flew north, then circled, hovering, as the cattle came to water.

Joanna, at the head of the horse herd, pushed the buckskin faster, hoping the birds had sense enough to stay in the air. A stampede, here, would be disastrous — animals bogged down, horses unable to find their footing, falling, and crushing riders.

"Not here," she muttered. "Please not here," and sighed in relief when a backward look showed the herd moving slowly on past the *playa* and the station house that huddled against the mountainside.

Six months before she had arrived at this very spot, innocent, unprepared for the havoc that lay ahead. How different it looked now! What a twisted road one traveled in the course

119

of a lifetime. What was it she'd said to Angus? That it might be possible to find beauty even in a place such as this. Well, she had been right. Not only had she discovered beauty, but she had found a friend, a man whose kiss had awakened a longing in her for something more than friendship. Angus! Where was he now, she wondered.

She squinted against the glare, saw the *playa* shimmering like glass, the stark, golden sides of the mountains, and the mile-long herd pushing steadily toward California. Happiness rose in her, a great joy like the sound of trumpets or the music of flying cranes. She had done this! Against all odds, she had made this vision into reality. Joanna O'Keefe, twenty-four years old and *en route* to California.

Ellis cut short her moment of glory. He pulled alongside, his face set. "Get 'em moving. The east-bound is due pretty soon, and we'd best be a couple miles away when it comes."

In her excitement she'd forgotten about the train. Now she looked west down the narrow bracelet of track. Nothing yet. But soon. Perhaps too soon. She pointed the buckskin at the tracks and felt his hesitation, his instinctive caution at being asked to cross a thing he'd never seen and couldn't understand. There had been no difficulty with the *remuda* so far, but all it would take was one wrong move from their leader, and the whole bunch would spook.

She steadied him with legs and voice, let him look at the source of his fright, then urged him across. Behind them, the horses, flanked by Juan and Ellis, followed, some jumping, some attempting to turn back, but being hazed relentlessly forward.

"Take 'em on outta here!" Ellis called, then turned back to the approaching cattle, the trail-wise Rupert in the lead.

Joanna set the pace toward the valley to the south. No time to lose, no time for self-congratulation. She kept the buckskin at a controlled lope, and searched for the safest way around fallen boulders, the ever-present cactus, and crumbling banks of treacherous washes. It was hard riding and dangerous, but there was a kind of glory in it that was far removed from anything she'd ever felt. This was where she belonged — in this immense country, on the back of a fine horse, the wind in her face, the drum beat of hoofs like the beating of her heart. This was the dream she had never dared to dream, this the freedom Alex had spoken of and that had been denied her because she was a woman. A freedom different from household drudgery, and all the more precious because she had fought for it and won. Surprising herself, she threw back her head and laughed.

And then, from the corner of her eye, she caught the glint of sun on metal. Far off, but coming fast, the east-bound train snaked toward them, a lethal toy. She didn't dare stop to see how the boys were doing. There was a job to be done. Abruptly her laughter ceased. She set her mouth in a grim line and rode on.

The valley sloped downhill, then leveled off on a broad, mesquite-covered plain. Now there were the trees to dodge, branches that whipped at her face, tore at her clothes. She slowed the buckskin, hoping the rest wouldn't run over them, wishing again that Angus was here, steady, reliable, clear-headed. But he'd gone off without so much as a word.

She heard the whistle of the train, but it seemed far away, too far to cause concern to her or the horses. Up ahead, she spotted a tank and a rough corral, and headed for them. Half the bunch followed her inside. The rest split off at the gate and ran, some back the way they'd come, others stampeding out into the valley. Without hesitation, she went after those that were headed toward the tracks. Too frightened to utter the curses that rose to her lips, she bent low over the buckskin's neck to keep from being knocked out of the saddle by the low branches. All that was needed to set the approaching cattle off was a glimpse of these frightened animals running flat out and straight to hell.

Not wanting to panic them further, she swung wide, closer to the tracks and parallel with them. "Come on!" she urged her mount. "Come on!"

He was tiring. She could feel his breath coming hard through the saddle leathers, feel the hammering of his heart as he labored to increase his pace. Even so, it seemed like an hour before he came abreast of the leaders, and then she wondered, could she push them? Would they follow, if she pulled ahead? Damned critters, always looking for an excuse to spook, always picking the worst time to do it, like now with the rumble of the oncoming train loud in her ears even over the pounding hoofs.

Desperate, she fumbled with the chin strap of her hat, pulled it off, and, yelling at the top of her lungs, waved it in the faces of the startled leaders. As she hoped, they shied away in terror, bunching up as they turned south and away from danger. Obviously, they were tiring, too. The pace slowed imperceptibly at first, and then, their panic forgotten, they dropped to a slow trot.

"Oh no," she told them, a glance over her shoulder showing the engine, its cowcatcher like a yawning mouth clearly visible. "Get going!" She waved her hat again, and the herd thundered over the edge of the first slope. Once out of sight of the train, she'd let them settle. And maybe, by then, someone would be able to help her.

She could have used Angus's help. If he'd been here, this near disaster might have been avoided. Instead, she'd handled it alone. She shuddered at the thought of what could have happened — horses, legs and backs broken, sprawled along the tracks, her own mount falling with her out of sheer exhaustion. She slammed her hat back on her head and reined in her imagination. No time for inventing troubles when she had troubles enough. She headed down the slope and, talking steadily, began to move the now calmed animals back toward the corral.

Juan met her at the gate of the corral she had used earlier. "*Señora,* stay!" he called to her. "I go back to help." He pointed to the cattle coming over the rise, and to the smoke from the engine clearly visible.

"Go ahead!" she called. "I'll make sure this gate holds." Then she curled her hands into fists and prayed.

They were all praying, or would, if they'd had time. The last bunch of stragglers cleared the gap and headed after the rest. Ellis wished he had four hands and eyes in the back of his head, but all he could do was keep moving, but not nearly as fast as he wanted.

"Jest don't go tootin' your horn," he muttered as he went down the first slope. He'd seen it happen. Some damn' fool engineer, who didn't know the first thing about handling live-stock, blasting a greeting, and in two minutes there was noth-ing to greet, just a cloud of dust and cattle headed for the hills.

Juan was making a circle toward the rear. A good kid. He'd make a top hand one day. And as for the lady boss, she had just proved herself again. There she was, the *remuda* secure, and there was water, scented by the cattle that increased their pace. He pulled aside to let them crowd to the edge, while the others swung wide and surrounded the little tank.

"Now toot your damn' head off!" Juan shouted at the sound of the whistle, and, catching sight of Joanna's smile, waved to her.

She felt her heart slow to normal and let out a sigh. Railroads were vital, were progress, yet, here, they could also be a dangerous enemy. It seemed there was danger everywhere.

Angus and Deering came through the pass and saw the herd grazing below. For the last few hours Angus had been going over the scene of the killing in his mind. Murder was the more accurate description. He'd stood there and seen his neighbor gun down two men with no more emotion than if they'd been pack rats, and he'd said nothing, then or now. Worse, he himself had shot another, justifiably, it was true, but cold-blooded murder was a thing he'd never witnessed, never wanted to see again.

He surveyed the scene in the valley — chuck wagon, *remuda,* and Joanna's white tent. What would she say when she knew?

"What'll we tell them?" he asked.

Deering smiled. "We don't have to tell them anything. We went after the horses. And if you're worried about the woman . . . don't be. She'd understand in a minute."

"I don't know. . . ." Angus wiped his face on his sleeve.

"I do. Unless you have the need to confess."

"Damn it, man," he began, then stopped, frustrated. He was as bad as a murderer himself. What would she think of that?

"Look at it this way. You saved my life back there. If you have to blab, she'll understand that. But frankly, I'd be happier if you kept the rest to yourself. They deserved what they got, and nobody's going to miss them. It's what happens to horse thieves, and everybody knows it."

Not so long ago the Scots had been called barbarians, but who were the barbarians now? He'd come here in the midst of many wars — with Indians, Mexicans, thieves, railroads run by scheming entrepreneurs. It was a raw, new country, and he was part of it whether he wished it or not.

In camp Joanna was waiting, a woman part and parcel of the country and its laws. And he, by God, was a McLeod with the blood of warriors in him. He pulled his hat down on his head and flashed a look at Deering.

"Let's go!" he said.

Chapter Eighteen

Joanna's head ached, as much from tension as anything else, and she was remembering her feelings when she had awakened and Angus was nowhere to be found, how she'd needed him later, but had fended for herself. As usual, she thought, setting her chin. Obviously, he couldn't be relied on any more than the others. And, for a while that morning, she had actually believed she was halfway in love with him. Well, she'd been strong for Alex, but she had no intention of making a habit of it. From now on, she was keeping her strength for herself.

"I wondered where you'd gone," she said, when he stopped at the door to her tent.

"Now you know, lass." But not all of it.

"I wish you'd told me you were leaving." Her voice carried a hint of petulance that made him oddly happy. So she'd worried about him!

"Does that mean you missed me?" he asked lightly.

Could she tell him how the world had turned to a still-life peopled with cardboard characters? Could she say she felt cut off, as if a part of her was missing, or that she was tired of being a nursemaid to every man she met? The pain in her temples grew worse. She'd only make a fool of herself groping for words.

She said: "I could've used your help," and hated the sound of it, so opposite from the truth.

"My help," he repeated foolishly, feeling as if she'd slapped him, then knowing a surge of anger at her and at himself. So that was all he meant to her — a slave, a rider, some-

126

one to be used when necessary. And he'd thought he was so much more. "Next time I'll be sure to ask your permission, before I do anything, *Missus O'Keefe*," he said, and walked away before anger and hurt pride got the better of him.

He stumbled on a rock, but kept walking out beyond the circle of light from Tino's fire. For a penny he'd be gone from this place. For two pennies he'd tell her what he thought of her and her cursed plans, her green eyes that lured a man on until he made a jester of himself.

"Slow down, man!" John caught up with him, took one look at his face, and smothered a laugh. A lover's quarrel. He'd wondered how soon that would happen.

"Be damned to you and this place!" Angus threw the words over his shoulder and kept walking. "Have you ever asked yourself what we're doin' here? What it's all comin' to? Us driving wild beasts to slaughter, when we could be sitting beside Gare Loch, watching the mist in the crags and never a worry about what was coming? Have you, man?"

John put an arm around his brother's shoulders. "There's times I've been close to despair, like when I wrote and asked for help. And then, there's times when something happens, maybe only a wee something that brings me to my senses. Forget it, Angus. She'll come 'round."

"I'll nae be used. By her, or anyone else."

John turned serious. "She's done as much or more than any of us. That's not using."

"So now you're her defender?"

"I'm talking sense had you the wit to hear it. She's nae using you is all I mean. The way I understood, we're all in this together, you, me, the lass. Though to tell the truth, I expected you'd marry her and leave me out of it."

"I'd as soon marry the English queen."

"And spend your life regretting it." John pulled out his

127

pipe and stuck the stem between his teeth. "The lass rode like a trooper all day. She's tired. Maybe doesn't know what she's saying. And so are you, probably." He paused. "They're dead, I expect?"

Angus nodded, relieved to admit it. "Shot down like rabbits and left to rot."

"Aye. Deering's a hard man, but a just one." He struck a match, puffed on the pipe until he got it going. "Best put it out of your head. It's the way things are here. And get some sleep."

"I'll nae be sleeping outside her door!"

John swallowed another chuckle. "I don't recall her asking you in the first place. Cheer up. We've a long way to go, and bad feelings won't help. Besides, things always look better in the morning."

Everything had turned upside down, Angus thought. Here was his brother, the doom-sayer, telling *him* how to feel, holding Joanna up as a paragon, when only a month before she'd been an addle-pated female incapable of intelligent thought. He spun on his heel and stalked off.

"Be damned to you both," he muttered as he lay down in his blankets and waited for sleep.

What had she done? Joanna lay awake, her head pounding, her heart sore. Angus's face danced before her in the darkness, hurt, angry, uncompromising. Why had she said what she did when she'd meant the opposite? Why had she resorted to deceit? Because, she decided glumly, she was a woman, and women were taught never to speak their minds, particularly as regarded their true feelings.

Having her say about the business had been shocking enough, a departure from all of society's rules, and she had found it exhilarating, but, when it came to a verbal exchange

128

concerning her inner confusion over Angus, she'd backed away, mumbled something cruel and idiotic, and had insulted him.

Tears ran down her cheeks, and the pain in her head increased. She hadn't slept at all when the pre-dawn racket told her another day had begun.

Tino looked at her ashen face with concern. "*Signora,* what is it?"

"My head." And feelings of loathing for herself that she couldn't talk about.

"Sit!" He dragged out a small stool, handed her a tin mug of coffee, then burrowed in his medicine chest. Returning, he poured a white powder in her tin mug. "Drink," he said.

"Joanna!" John said, coming up and stopping beside her. "Are you all right?" She looked, he thought, worse than his brother, if that were possible.

She shook her head slowly. "No. Headache. It'll pass."

He resisted the urge to remind her about women who insisted on going on the trail. She was miserable enough without his adding to it. "Ride with Tino, lass," he said. "You've been working too hard."

"I might." Even her jaws ached, probably because she'd been grinding her teeth all night.

They looked up at the sound of a trotting horse and strange voices at the edge of camp.

"Henry! Francesca! It's the Colonel and his daughter," he told Joanna. "Come to get their horse, no doubt. I sent Juan with a message last night."

Just what she didn't need. A social call. Slowly she got to her feet and walked toward the visitors.

"The red dun is Francesca's. El Cobre, she calls him, and I know she's as glad to have him back as I am." The Colonel was shaking hands with Deering. "We thought we'd come out . . . see how you folks were getting along . . . take the horse back ourselves." He turned, seeing Joanna. "My dear, what a pleasure."

She forced a smile. "Good to see you again, Colonel."

Always observant, he noticed her pallor and the pain in her eyes. "What is it?" he asked.

"Headache."

Swiftly he made up his mind. "You'll come back to the house with us. No," — he raised his hand at her protest — "I insist. A hot bath, a good rest in a decent bed, and you'll be fine. Don't worry. We'll catch up with the boys when you're better, I'll see to that. Francesca!"

He gestured at his daughter who was talking to John, one hand on his arm and her heart on her sleeve.

Why Francesca had fallen in love with this stone-faced man was a mystery even to herself, but there it was. John McLeod never seemed to pay her any more attention than was polite, which was also mysterious, because young, pretty women were a rarity, and she was both with her Mexican mother's black hair and oval face and her father's startling blue eyes. And now there was another beautiful woman for her to contend with — the O'Keefe widow who had the advantage of being near John day after day. She frowned as she heard her father calling, then flashed a dazzling smile at John. "I hope you'll have good weather," she said. "And good luck. Please come see us when you get back, and let us know all about it. You will, won't you?"

"I will, indeed." He found himself smiling back. Such a pretty thing she was! Odd he hadn't noticed before. He offered her his arm. "Let's see what your father wants."

Angus, watching the scene from a distance, noticed how Francesca looked at his brother and Harrington's concern for

Joanna. *Women!* he thought bitterly. Always making up to whatever male suited their needs at the moment. And he'd deluded himself into believing that Joanna felt as he did, that the future belonged to them. Well, let her go off with the Colonel. Let his brother stumble after the girl like some gangling puppy. He'd see the drive through, then say his farewells, and be on a ship bound for Scotland. And good riddance to this place filled with barbarians.

Without a word he took the horse Juan brought up, threw on the heavy saddle, and cinched it tight without his usual gentleness. Then he caught himself. Taking out anger on animals wasn't his way. "Sorry, old boy," he said softly and rubbed the horse's neck before loosening the girth. "I'm just frazzled this morning."

He swung up and watched Harrington assist Joanna into the buggy. She looked, he had to admit, far from happy, as unlike Francesca and his brother as possible. Francesca had brought her own saddle, a proper lady's one, and John was giving her a boost onto the big red horse while she smiled and chattered, seemingly unaware of his admiration.

"Now the boot's on the other foot," he said to himself. "And a proper fit it may be." Still, he wasn't in any mood to tease his brother. He wanted a hard ride, no time to brood. Work was always a sure cure for misery of any kind. He wheeled around and went looking for Ellis.

Chapter Nineteen

"Are you sure you want to continue on to California?" The Colonel put the mare into a fast trot, then bent his head toward Joanna.

Once more she gritted her teeth — against the jouncing of the buggy, the dual pain inside. "Yes," she said. "It's history, you see." Angus's words again. They seemed such a part of her.

"What a fascinating thought!"

"Yes," she agreed, "fascinating." Closing her eyes, she didn't speak again until they drew up in the ranch yard.

"Here we are, and welcome. Francesca's ahead of us, unless I'm mistaken. Rides like a Tartar, that girl." The pride in his voice was evident — in his daughter and in his house.

Joanna opened her eyes, winced at the bright sunlight, and saw an adobe house of such grandeur that she blinked again. There was a portal shaded by cottonwood trees, the supporting posts vine covered, the carved wooden doors gracious and welcoming. It was a house such as she'd dreamed of — shade dappled, its wings stretched out to visitors like arms.

"It's lovely!" Already she felt her pain receding, curiosity taking its place. Oh, given money enough and time, what she couldn't build back at the ranch headquarters! And live alone in what she'd designed while old age overtook her, she thought miserably.

"It's built like my dead wife's house in Hermosillo," he said, tucking her hand in the crook of his arm. "She was unhappy away from her family, her house and garden, so I

132

recreated them."

Dead? She tilted her head to look up at his leonine face and hooded blue eyes. "I'm sorry."

"And I. But she left me Francesca."

"She's beautiful."

He bent his head in assent. "And knows it."

The carved doors opened, and Francesca stood watching them, her eyes glittering. "I beat you!"

"So you did. And now take Joanna to her room. We'll talk later."

"Yes, Papa." Her words were demure, her attitude less so. "Come." She tugged at Joanna's arm and led her down a stone-floored hall.

Now she had the chance to ask the questions that had been roiling in her head all the way home. Now she could ask about John, but with discretion. If, indeed, this widow was her opponent, she would have to be clever, spinning a web of illusion so as to disarm her.

"This is so kind of you," Joanna said. "I was beginning to wonder if I'd ever have a bath again."

Francesca looked at her with curiosity. "How do you manage things? Alone with all those men."

"They're a good bunch. I even have my own tent to sleep in." And Angus guarding her. But not last night. Without warning, she burst into tears.

Francesca opened a door and pulled her inside. "Is it your head? Does it hurt badly? Don't cry." In spite of her worries, she was frightened to see this woman weeping as if she couldn't stop.

The girl's concern touched her, and Joanna gulped down a sob. "I'm just being foolish. Forgive me." She thought that perhaps she'd lived in the world of men too long, reining in her emotions, avoiding that part of herself that was most feminine, merely to belong.

"It's not foolish to cry when you have to. Tell me." Francesca sat down on the edge of the bed and pulled Joanna beside her.

It would be nice to have a friend, even this young, probably innocent girl. It would be a relief to speak her mind — her *other* mind — the one she'd been ignoring. Joanna took a deep breath. "Last night I said something stupid, and Angus got mad. I . . . I hurt his feelings without meaning to, and now I don't know what to do."

Francesca's heart jumped in relief. "Angus?"

"John's brother. He . . . he's been my support all along. Not like John."

"Don't you like John?" Her voice rose as if she were ready to defend him.

"I do. It's just . . . he can be difficult. Always putting rocks in the way of progress. Very aggravating, especially when you can see what has to be done and can't get him to admit it." She looked at Francesca, who was staring at her lap, her fingers pleating the folds of her skirt, and suddenly she understood. The poor girl, motherless, most likely lonely, had a crush on John who wouldn't recognize it if she stood up and bit him. "He's a good man," she said. "Just hard to figure sometimes. How long have you known him?"

"Since he first came. He stopped here with . . . with your husband. I thought he was wonderful, but he never seemed to notice me."

"And you care for him?"

Francesca bit her lip, then nodded. "I think so. Yes."

"What does your father say?"

"He doesn't know."

The image of John assisting the girl into the saddle came to her. Perhaps he wasn't as immune as he appeared. Certainly he'd been attentive that morning. Her headache was fading, whether from Tino's medicine or the fact that she was distracted from her own problems, she didn't know. She said: "We need a plan."

"A plan?" Francesca's blue eyes widened.

"Some way to get him to notice you. That's what you want, isn't it?"

"Oh yes," she whispered. "Yes."

"You're beautiful, you know," Joanna said, and watched as a blush colored the girl's cheeks.

"I look like my mother. She died after I was born."

"It must have been hard, growing up here by yourself."

She shook her head. "I had Papa. And Antonia, my mother's maid. And my horses. Then I went away to school for two years, but I was lonely. I wanted to be here. Can you understand that?"

Here there were grass-covered valleys, painted hills, the sound of wind, the music of birds. Here, violence and peace, chaos and order existed simultaneously, enhancing the beauty with the threat of extinction. Here was awareness. Here was home.

"Yes," she whispered, reaching for the girl's slender hand. "Yes, I can. Now . . . about that plan."

The Colonel lived well, Joanna decided as she leaned against the carved back of her chair and sipped wine from a heavy goblet. They had been served bean soup, roast chicken, a salad of young lettuces grown by Harrington in the warmth of the inner courtyard, and the accompanying conversation had been intelligent, but light enough not to interfere with the pleasure of eating.

"This has been wonderful," she told him. "I'm grateful to you both."

135

"And your headache?"

"Gone." She raised her glass. "Thanks to you."

"I've been thinking." He raised his own glass in response, thinking that she looked perfect in the candlelight.

"What about?"

"It's been several years since I've been on a drive. Would you object if I joined you? At least as far as Yuma?"

It was her chance — hers and Francesca's. Avoiding the girl's eyes she answered. "Of course, you can! We'd be glad of your expertise. And I'd be glad to have Francesca's company."

Startled, he raised black brows. "Francesca! I wasn't suggesting that she accompany us."

"Oh, I'd love to!" Francesca leaned across the table. "Say I can, Papa. Please! We'd have such fun, and Joanna sleeps in her own tent at night. I could, too, couldn't I?" She looked pleadingly at her new friend.

"Sure you can." Joanna sipped at her wine to keep from laughing, then turned to the Colonel. "She'll be with me and safe. It'll be an adventure." At those words, she thought of Angus again. What was he doing now? Still nursing his anger toward her?

Harrington looked from one expectant face to the other, seeking an out but not finding one. Francesca was his jewel, his only child, whom he'd nurtured, cherished, protected just as he had her mother. But suddenly she was no longer helpless. Overnight, she'd turned into a woman, and a determined one at that. He cleared his throat.

"It's a hard ride."

She laughed. "Stuff! I learned to ride from you. I can ride all day and dance all night . . . when there is a dance." Her face fell, remembering the few dances she'd been to, always with Antonia as chaperon, always looking for John,

136

but never finding him.

Her father read her disappointment and believed he understood. What kind of a life was it for her here, away from all the things young girls adored — music, dancing, clothes? Perhaps he'd been too protective. He sighed. "All right. But we will only go as far as Tucson. You can stay with your aunt and go to lots of parties, until I get back. How's that? Better?"

She wanted to laugh and cry at the same time. Even driving the herd they'd reach the city in a week, and what did she care about parties without John? "It's not long enough," she wailed.

"It's quite long enough," he said sternly. "You'll be happy to see a house again by then, believe me."

Joanna shot a warning glance across the table. A lot could happen in a week. "Then we'll be sure to make use of every minute, won't we, Francesca?" she said.

Chapter Twenty

John, riding drag, saw the three riders coming, one leading an extra horse, two cattle dogs loping behind. He thought they looked like a party of Englishmen out for a day's sport — Francesca in a dark green riding habit perched sidesaddle, and Joanna, her broad-brimmed hat set at a rakish angle, while the Colonel rode like the cavalry officer he'd been, standing up in the stirrups. They slowed as they came up to him.

"I've brought company!" Joanna said, laughing.

Did she always have to turn work into play? "Is it a party, then?"

"Stick-in-the-mud!" She shot him a hard glance. "We can use the Colonel's help."

"And her?" He nodded at Francesca.

"She's to look at. Maybe she'll take your mind off things." Joanna rode off, leaving him with his mouth open, wondering how it was that he always said the wrong thing, and she always made the most of it. He didn't envy his brother, who was still brooding over whatever had happened between them. The woman was a handful, no doubt about it. Still, she'd been right about Francesca. A man could do worse than spend his time looking at that face.

He nodded at the Colonel. "Decided to come along for the ride?"

"A man gets to miss the old days. Gets soft sitting at home."

Counting his money, John thought, but all he said was: "Glad to have you."

Joanna felt her high spirits evaporating as she and Francesca caught up with the *remuda*. What could she say to Angus? What would he say to her, if anything? Even an exchange of fighting words would be better than antagonistic silence.

"Don't worry." Francesca had read her mind. "He can't stay mad forever."

"He's a proud man."

"All men are. Women aren't allowed to be. Except when we get old, but then it's too late. Why don't you just tell him the truth?"

"Because I'm not sure what the truth is, or what I feel. I thought one thing, and said another, and how can I explain that?"

"You just did. But I wouldn't try it on him till tonight. Let's just turn this horse loose and ride for fun, and not worry. Isn't it a gorgeous day?"

"It is, and you're right." Joanna tilted her head to look up at the sky, a clear, cloudless blue. Around them the mountains were golden in the sunlight, and the valley was dotted with the white plumes of blooming broom that tossed in the slight breeze.

"There's Juan," she said. "He can take the horse, and we'll go find Tino and help him with supper. Angus will have to wait."

"But not too long." Francesca cocked a delicate eyebrow, appearing sophisticated far beyond her years.

John, Joanna thought, was in for a surprise. As for her own problem, it would have to be dealt with, and the sooner the better. Although she hated to admit it, she missed his friendship, his conversation, the warmth of his eyes when he looked at her. She wasn't being disloyal to Alex's memory. All that lay behind her. She was here now and lonely in spite of

139

Francesca's company. Had she lost him forever because of a few harsh words? With a sigh, she admitted the possibility, and with a stab of pain in her heart she admitted that, for the first time in her life, she was in love.

Terrill watched the group around the campfire with a smoldering resentment that bordered on hatred. There they all were, playing a game, instead of tending to business. That was how the rich always behaved, as if life were fun instead of day-to-day grubbing to earn a dollar, and switching partners when they got bored or just for the hell of it.

He finished his dinner and walked off, unable to face any of them. What made them more deserving than he? It was all a matter of luck, no more. With any luck it could have been him sitting there flirting with the lady boss, instead of saddling up to ride night herd. Was it his fault his old man had run off and left him and his ma to fend for themselves? Was it his fault his mother had had enough and had hanged herself in the barn? He'd been eight, and he'd cut her down and buried her in a shallow hole on the Texas plains. From then on, he'd been on his own, drifting, stealing just to quiet the hunger in his belly, to take out his anger on somebody worse off than he was — other drifters, poor Mexicans, and, once in a while, some rancher with more livestock than could be counted in three months of gathering.

He remembered the afternoon he'd ridden up to the Circle MC headquarters, two steps ahead of a horse-stealing charge, and found those losers — the foreigner, McLeod, and the skinny Texas lawyer, O'Keefe — trying their damnedest to do what neither was cut out for. Scotty had been there, and the greaser cook, and they'd welcomed him gladly. He'd worked. By God, he'd worked, and, if once in a while he ran off a few beefs or a horse or two across the line, where he had friends, he'd earned it.

Then O'Keefe had found Micaela. She was a whore, but all women were, given the right circumstances, even his mother who, more than once, had let a stranger into her bed for money. Even though Micaela had been a whore, he'd wanted her from the first day — all frightened eyes and slender as a whip, except where her breasts poked out of her shift like two lush peaches ready for the tasting. He'd watched her, stalked her, but she was wary. In her life with the Apaches she'd learned a trick or two. But he'd caught her once, laughed as she fought him with a considerable strength, laughed and forced her down and almost had her except she was quick and caught him in the groin. And as he had rolled off, gasping, she'd hit him in the head with a rock. The bitch! Even now he could taste his anger — and his rising lust. He wasn't good enough even for a Mexican whore!

Out of the corner of his eye he caught a glimpse of something white at the edge of the *remuda*. The other bitch, her with the face like one of the *santos* the Mexicans prayed to in their churches. She'd been hanging around John for two days now, begging for it, and him too blind to notice.

At the sound of his footsteps Francesca turned, her smile fading as she saw not John, whom she had hoped would follow her, but the man Joanna had said was trouble waiting to happen.

"You oughtn't to be walkin' around by yourself," Terrill said. That was a fact. Out here, on the far side of the *remuda* and in the long shadows of night, the campfire was only a distant light, the voices of the others far away.

He'd scared her. He saw her hands tremble as she clasped them together in front of her, but, when she answered, her voice was steady. "I guess I'll be going back, now."

"I'll go with you. Just to make sure." He grabbed her arm above the elbow and felt her flinch away from him. "Don't," he said.

"Don't what?" She was more frightened than she'd ever been, reading his intentions in his posture, but fright fueled her anger. How dare he touch her like he owned her? How dare he bring his face close to hers so she could smell his foul breath, his lust. "Let go."

"Act nice," he said. "Like I was him. You'd give it to him quick enough. I seen how you look at him. Like a whore."

She tried to pull free, but he grabbed her other arm. Now she was pinned against him, twisting her face away, writhing in his grip. She was going to be raped by this creature who stank of sweat and rotten teeth and cattle dung. Her scream split the night in two, startling the horses dozing in the *remuda,* echoing off the mountains like a bell.

"Francesca!" John pulled his pistol and listened for the scream to repeat, but all that followed was silence, deep and menacing.

They were all on their feet, hampered by the tricks sound played driven by the wind through the bowl of the valley.

Rain was making his last circle around the cattle and, even in the dusk, was close enough to see the struggling figures. His first impression was that it was Joanna locked in Terrill's arms. He spurred his horse, reached them in a few seconds, and jumped off, catching sight of a white face, eyes wide with terror.

"What in hell are you doing? Let her go!"

He didn't expect an answer and didn't get one. What he got was a punch in the jaw as Terrill spun around swinging.

Francesca took advantage of the diversion and took off, leaping rocks and dodging branches, her heart pounding so hard it threatened to cut off her breath. Halfway back, she ran

142

full tilt into John's arms.

"Are you all right? What happened?" Even in his excitement he noticed she was pleasant to hold, fitting into the curve of his arm as if she'd been molded there.

"Terrill. He. . . ." She couldn't say more, and didn't have to.

"Where?"

"By the horses."

"Go on back," he ordered. "And stay there. I'll take care of the bastard."

Rain was getting the worst of it, but he was still on his feet when John stepped in, grabbed Terrill's arm, and landed a punch to his gut and another to his head, felling him. It was an effort to keep from kicking the man like the dog he was, an act of control to keep from murdering him, even half-conscious and helpless. After a minute he said: "You're fired. Get your gear and get out."

Dimly his words played through. Fired. And on account of a whore. "You owe me back pay." It was hard talking through the haze in his head and the split in his lip. Terrill got up slowly and spat out blood and one of his teeth.

"You owe me," he repeated.

"Aye. Come up to the wagon, when you've got your things."

Rain's face was ghastly in the light of the rising moon — one eye turning purple and blood pouring out of his nose. "Sorry, boss," he mumbled. "He was . . . he was after the girl." He choked on the blood and stopped, swaying on his feet.

"Come on." John put an arm around him. "You did right. Now, we'll get you fixed up. Scotty can take Terrill's shift. And no apologies. He got what he deserved."

Back at the campfire, Angus was thinking, *it could have*

143

been Joanna. It could have been her helpless in that bastard's grip. Ah, hell! Love wasn't an easy thing to get over. Maybe a man never forgot the first one, just took second best and made a life and kept his memories in his shirt pocket to take out and dream on when he got the chance. Except he, Angus McLeod, had never settled for second best in his life. By God, he'd have his say. If not tonight, then soon.

That's how they were, the rich — closing ranks against outsiders, throwing their weight around like they were gods, kicking the shit out of anybody they chose, even over a woman! And that bastard, John, had cracked a rib with his last kick to his gut. He could feel the grabbing pain when he took a breath, when he threw his saddle over one of his two geldings.

He wanted to make them pay. He wanted to see them grovel. Most of all he wanted to see the lady boss's face when she heard the truth. It was all her fault anyhow — her and her snotty friends. He didn't risk mounting his horse, not with the pain snaking through him. He'd do that after. When he was out of their sight. And he'd ride away laughing, even if it killed him.

"It's not broken, but you came close." Joanna packed Rain's nose with cotton in an effort to stop the bleeding, then gently explored the bone. He'd have a black eye by morning, but there was nothing she could do about that. "Guess you were lucky," she said.

"I should've killed him." Rain's voice was thick. "He's no good. Never was."

"Well, now we're rid of him. And thanks to you, Francesca's all right."

John and the Colonel had taken the nearly hysterical girl

144

to the tent. Perhaps some good would come out of evil, after all.

Joanna repacked the medicine chest and gave it to Tino to put away, then lifted out the money box and began to count what was owed to Terrill. Abruptly she turned to Angus and thrust the money at him. "Here. You handle it." She sounded brusque even to herself, and a look at Angus's face told her she'd done it again. "I didn't mean it like it sounded," she said.

"Like a harpy." He stopped her retort with a gesture. "Nay, lass, we'll not argue now. There's been enough trouble for one night."

So he was still angry, and once again she'd spoken without thinking. It was this life that was changing her, drawing a veil over the softness of her emotions, teaching her to command though she hadn't asked to learn.

"I. . . ." She was interrupted by Terrill, appearing like a gargoyle at the edge of the flickering light.

"I'll take my pay."

"You'll take it and be out of here." Angus handed over the bills. "And if I see you again, you'll not get off as easy."

Slowly, deliberately, Terrill counted the money, and, when finished, he looked at Joanna, a sneer twisting his split lip.

"You think I'm dirt, don't you? You think you and your fancy friends're too good for the likes of me. Well, I'll tell you something you oughta know, and then you ask yourself who's better. You ask yourself who's the father of that Mexican brat? Who couldn't keep his hands off the little bitch, and all the time orderin' me around like I was trash? Ask anybody about it, Missus High And Mighty. Ask anybody about your husband, and then tell me if what I done was any worse." He spat at her feet, and she stared at the bloody saliva, numb, horrified, unable to assimilate what she had heard.

With a roar, Angus swung and knew a deep, animal satisfaction as his fist connected with Terrill's jaw, knocking him back against the wheel of the chuck wagon.

"I'll cut out your nasty tongue! I'll cut you in two and leave the parts for the wolves!"

In spite of his earlier beating, Terrill wasn't licked. He'd grown up fighting on the streets. He lifted his knee and got Angus in the groin, and landed an extra punch before he went down. The hell with the pain in his ribs. He'd lived through worse. Right now, he was going to pound this bastard's head to mush, like he wanted to do to them all.

Pinned down, rendered almost helpless from the agony between his legs, Angus reached for Terrill's neck. The son-of-a-bitch fought dirty, but he'd be damned if he'd lie here whimpering, not after what he had just said to Joanna.

Joanna stood transfixed and watching, listening, horrified at the sounds of the fight, like two animals grunting, locked together in a death struggle. Then the threat to Angus broke through her shock. Without hesitation, she drew her pistol and advanced on the two men. "Stop now, or, by God, I'll kill you, Terrill Fox."

Even in his rage he heard her, heard the click as she cocked the hammer, saw her feet planted firmly on the ground beside him. She meant it. The bitch would shoot, and he'd be dead and buried here. He gave a final thump to Angus's head and pushed himself away.

"Shit!" He shook himself like a dog and held his hands away from himself. "Don't shoot."

"Just get on your horse and get!"

In his experience, women with guns couldn't be trusted. They were just as likely to blow you away without warning as not. "All right. I'm going." It hurt to talk, to move, but he backed away slowly and crawled up on his horse, though the pain made him want to puke. He'd been crazy to get mixed up with this bunch. Rustling paid better, and a man was his own boss. Well, he'd make them pay, every last one of them. Somehow, he'd find a way. "I'll get you," he mumbled, unwilling to leave without bluster.

The bullet blew off his hat into the night, and Joanna advanced on him with fury written all over her. "The next one'll be between your eyes." She meant it.

He turned his horse and moved off into the dark, not stopping to look for his hat.

147

Chapter Twenty-One

Joanna replaced her pistol in its holster and choked down her rage. They had all known, every one of them, Angus, too, and they'd let her go on clutching the memory of Alex to herself like a child clutches a doll. And the baby! How she'd loved the little thing. Alex's baby! She should have known. Should have been able to tell in the instant she saw that red hair. But she'd been so trusting. And see where that had gotten her — to this lonely valley and the hateful truth out of the mouth of a no-good drifter.

The night whirled around her, and she wondered if this, too, wasn't illusion, if she wouldn't wake and find herself safe in her bed in Texas with the mockingbirds singing outside the window. But no, there they all were, those men she thought she knew, their faces blurred by the firelight, their eyes dark and secretive hollows above bearded cheeks. And there was Angus getting slowly to his feet and looking as if he'd rather be anywhere but here.

She started to go to him, out of habit, then checked herself. He was as bad as the rest, and she'd allowed herself to be deceived in her own weakness. Well, no more. Let him tend to his own wounds, and be damned to him. She had plenty of her own. Suddenly she realized she could not remain silent.

"How could you? How could you know and not tell me?" Her hands curled into fists, and she shoved them deep in her pockets.

He was seeing two of her, and his head ached as if it were about to fall off. He wished it would. Of all the times to pick for a showdown with this woman whose eyes were like hard pieces of jade, but whose voice trembled with what he realized was an almost unendurable hurt.

"Lass," he whispered.

"Don't you 'lass' me!" She was bitter now and deadly. "Don't any of you 'lass' me. You bunch of conspiring cowards. Don't you think you should have told me about my husband? Didn't I have the right to the truth? Or was it fun to watch me make a fool out of myself . . . the bereaved widow . . . the silly woman who'd fall to pieces if she knew?"

She stunned them. Not a one had the courage to look her in the face, not even the Colonel, whose mouth was a tight line, and whose eyes were fixed firmly on her feet.

"You, too," she hissed at him. "Don't tell me you had no idea. I bet the whole county knew about how the widow O'Keefe had taken in her husband's bastard. That's right. Bastard. Not a word usually used by ladies, is it? Shocks you, doesn't it? Well that's not half of the shock I just got. And from that son-of-a-bitch, Terrill. Think about that. How none of you had the guts to tell me. Just a no-good saddle tramp."

Only Tino broke the silence, coming to her side and putting a gnarled hand on her arm. *"Signora,"* he said gently. *"Signora.* Sometime in life we make mistake. We think what we do is right, but we think wrong. And we think this way because we no want to hurt nobody. You understand me?"

She didn't want to understand. She had to hold on to her anger or the tears would start, and she refused to give this jury of liars the pleasure of seeing her weep. She snatched her arm away. "What I see is that you're all guilty. You hoped to sweep this under the rug and never have to talk about it again, never have to ask yourselves if you'd been honest. Or, maybe, you all have your own bunch of bastards hidden out somewhere. It wouldn't surprise me. Nothing will ever surprise me

149

again. And the trouble is, I'm stuck with you and this damned cattle drive. I'll finish it, but for all I care you can go to hell in a handcart." Especially Angus. He who'd kissed her, lied to her, let her exist in simple-minded bliss. "That goes double for you," she said to him. "You're as bad as the rest, if not worse." Then she ran.

"I've never been so scared in my life! That awful man! He . . . he *smelled!*" Francesca was sitting up, wrapped inside her blankets, chattering like a blackbird, much to Joanna's dismay. "But John was wonderful. And he said he'd come with me to my aunt Felice's house, and stop on his way back from San Diego. So our plan is working in spite of everything, and I don't know how to thank you."

Joanna pulled off her boots, wishing in vain for silence. "That's good then," was all she said, but it was enough to alert Francesca.

"What's the matter? Are you and Angus still mad at each other? What happened out there? I heard a shot."

"I helped Terrill on his way."

"And?"

"Nothing. I'm just tired." She was a rag doll with the stuffing leaking out, a bird with a broken wing and no song left to sing. All she wanted was to put out the lamp and hold to herself in the dark. All she wanted was the oblivion of sleep so she wouldn't have to think or feel. They'd all known, even Clemmie, and they'd pitied her. It was their pity that hurt the worst, as if she'd been a child they needed to protect. And Angus had known all along. Even when he kissed her, he must have been feeling sorry for her in her innocence, and she, like any passionate woman, had misunderstood. What she felt now was shame. Now all the past conversations, the shocked faces made sense. She had been made a fool because of Alex.

Alex! The very name made her sick. She wanted to vomit. She wanted to pound the ground in a rage and scream and weep, but tears wouldn't come. She was dry-eyed, as if fury had burned away any hint of tears.

Slowly she bent down and blew out the lamp.

Chapter Twenty-Two

If Joanna hadn't been so miserable, the sight of the cañon, its rocky sides cut into a million twisted shapes by wind and rain, would have awed her. As it was, she saw it as yet another difficulty to be gotten through. Boulders the size of houses lay strewn on the rough floor and the narrow, winding trail, others balanced precariously overhead, threatening to slide off at any moment, startling the wary cattle and the horses in the *remuda* that were already spooked by the strangeness of the enclosure.

Angus had avoided her since the trouble three nights before, and Francesca had spent every free moment in John's company, leaving her with the Colonel who, it seemed, was courting her — a complication she neither needed nor desired. In her present state of mind that fluctuated between misery and bitter resentment, she had no idea how to respond to his subtle advances and what seemed his constant seeking of her company. She wanted to be alone to lick her wounds, to turn her face into the wind and let it blow away her thoughts.

No one, least of all herself, had taken the weaknesses of human nature into consideration when planning the cattle drive. Although bonded together in a common effort, individual foibles were becoming a factor that intruded on the major purpose. Small dramas were taking place within the large one, and she was too confused and heart-sore to solve problems or sort out difficulties.

It was with a sense of relief that she came to the mouth of the twisting cañon and looked down on the valley below. In the late afternoon the sand hills shimmered pink like the inside of a shell, and just visible behind a rough stand of mesquite and cottonwood branches was the river, a thread of gold.

The Colonel came up beside her. "A pretty scene," he remarked. "I've been told that this was all an ocean once. All underwater, if you can imagine such a thing. There was a party of geologists out last year. They told me these sand hills are full of fossils. Even brought out a couple of wagonloads. Odd-looking things . . . shells . . . fish . . . what have you. Perhaps, after supper, you and I can hunt for some."

She gave him a small smile, wishing he'd go away. But since the scene three nights before, he'd gone out of his way to stay with her, talk to her, attempt to bring her out of her depression. "Maybe," she said.

"You're still upset about the other night. They all did what they thought was best. For my part, I told you, I hardly knew your husband. Met him only once that I can remember. If you want my advice, you'll forget the whole thing and go on like it never happened."

"I can't. I keep wondering how I can trust my own judgment. How I could have been so stupid. So blind."

"A failure of human nature and quite common," he said. "We see only what we want."

She sighed. "Right now, all I see is that for much of my life I've been living a lie. Maybe I still am. I thought this drive was the solution to a problem and worked to make it happen. Now, I think I was simply deceiving myself. As usual."

"Actually, it's a brilliant idea, and you were quite right. You're an unusual woman, Joanna."

Something in his voice alerted her. In spite of her confusion, she realized he was probably about to make a proposal which would only complicate her life further.

153

"Let's go down," she said. She nudged her horse and moved away quickly, leaving him with nothing to do but follow.

Angus scowled at the pair as they disappeared over the brow of the hill and fought back his own jealousy. Being treated as a servant had been bad enough, but, ever since she'd found out about the deception, Joanna hadn't so much as looked at him. It was as if he no longer existed, as if he was a rock to be walked around, a tree to be avoided, and to make matters worse, Harrington was quite obviously courting her. Even John, caught up in admiration for Francesca, had noticed.

"Better settle your difficulties with the lass, or she'll be snapped up right under your nose," he'd said the night before when, for once, Francesca hadn't been attached to his arm.

"Mind your own bloody business for once," Angus retorted, struck by the fact that he had no idea how to make it right between them. For the first time in his life he didn't know how to proceed, what magic words to use to bring her to her senses.

If only he could get her alone — but she was wary, heading for her tent each night after supper, riding off in the morning with Harrington in attendance, and refusing even to glance at him. He consoled himself with the fact that the road to San Diego was a long one, and that, surely, somewhere between here and there, he'd have his chance to speak. If only the Colonel didn't speak first.

Something was wrong. Joanna's horse skittered sideways, shaking its head, kicking at its belly, at the same time that the *remuda* broke into a wild gallop. "What on earth?" was all she managed to ask before her horse put its head down and bucked, ran a few yards and bucked again, frenzied, out of control. Gamely, she held on, even though she felt as if her head was about to be snapped off, her body wrenched apart. "God help me," were the last words she uttered before the horse swapped ends. She hit the ground and lay unmoving, while around her horses and cattle took off in a mad stampede.

How long she lay unconscious, she didn't know. When she came to, it was late afternoon, and she was alone. The horizon whirled around her, and the mountains seemed to be doing a dance to the tune of the ringing in her ears. She closed her eyes, then opened them cautiously. "Better," she mumbled, and shut them again in the hope of making sense of her situation.

Her horse had gone crazy. She remembered that — and suddenly being thrown through the air. Then, nothing. Slowly she pushed herself into a sitting position. Nothing was broken, she decided, although she was one large ache, the worst part of which was her head.

Had the rest of them missed her? Were they out looking, or had disaster struck them all? She could sit here and hope to be found, or she could try to walk it, by following the trail left by the herd. She sat for a while until the world steadied and the mountains remained stationary in their places, then she clambered to her feet and stood breathing deeply. A few feet away, she saw her hat, squashed flat, and for a moment she felt nauseous. It could have been her lying there broken beyond recognition. It could have been any one of them. But where were they? Around her was silence, as if the earth were holding its breath, waiting for her to discover a secret, and the clues were in the churned-up ground that seemed to have been gouged by a gigantic plow from the looks of the broken stems of the feathery broom and creosote bushes, the trampled cholla with its fearsome barbs.

To walk or wait? Joanna didn't know, but she had never been one to sit idly and do nothing. She would walk westward, following the sun and the devastation, and sooner or later would find an answer, the cattle, the crew of men. Slowly she bent and picked up her hat, staggering as her dizziness returned, and with it the fear that she was more badly hurt than she had thought. If she walked on and passed out, they might never find her. The possibility that she might die out here was truly frightening. She hadn't finished what she'd started, and there was so much left to do! With an effort, she raised her head, threw back her shoulders, punched her hat into a caricature of its original shape, and began to walk.

"One. Two. One. Two." She kept herself moving by ordering her feet, keeping her eyes on the ground, uttering commands through bruised lips. Her misery over Alex's faithlessness and the deceits that had followed seemed like nothing compared to the ache of her body. Not a muscle was free of pain, and her head pounded in time with her steps. Her mouth and throat were parched, making even her few words difficult. She stumbled, then caught herself. No point thinking about water. There was none. "One. Two. One. Two." How much longer? How far to safety?

"Angus," she said, "Angus," and the thought of him and his deceit was too much to bear. She walked on, her vision blurred this time by tears.

"Angus."

By the time Rain, riding point, realized the danger, it was too late. He'd ridden into a stand of cholla, and the lead steers had followed. His horse bogged its head and bucked, while, behind him, the enraged steers, driven mad from the pain in their switching tails and sensitive muzzles, split off and ran, with the drags and the *remuda* following.

By a miracle, everyone came through without injury, even Chapo who'd been thrown into the middle of the stampeding cattle when his horse went berserk, and Rain, who would spend the next week picking barbs out of himself.

In all his life, Angus had never seen a disaster happen so quickly — horses running wild, cattle going off in all directions, men on foot scampering to the pathetic shelter of trees or boulders, while the ground beneath them shook, the air around them resonated from the bawling of terrified and helpless animals. By still another miracle, Angus's mount had escaped contact with the cholla, but, taking fright along with the rest, the horse had grabbed the bit in its teeth and ran after the others. Only after a mile had Angus regained control and circled back.

He found Deering, Ellis, Scotty, the Colonel, and Francesca still on horseback. The others were on foot, dust-covered and bruised. There was no sign of Joanna.

"Where is she?" he asked, anxiety rasping in his throat. "Where's Joanna?"

"Last I seen, she was riding the *remuda*," Ellis Jackson volunteered, a frown puckering the foreman's forehead. "Maybe she went after them. But we can't go look till we get hosses for all of us."

"She might be hurt." To hell with the horses, thought Angus. He was ready to take off on a search, and he headed out.

Harrington, characteristically, took charge. "Those of us with horses will find the others' mounts. But before we do anything, I suggest we check our own for cactus. It's treacherous stuff, as we just saw."

Francesca pulled a comb out of one deep pocket. "And if you find any, use this. It's the only way to pull them out without getting stuck yourselves." She tossed it to John who looked at her with admiration.

"Clever lass," he said.

"A trick I learned a long time ago. And worth remembering out here." She flashed him a smile. "While you do that, I'll go look for Joanna."

"You should not be going off on your own," John put in. "We should all stay together."

"You forget," she told him, "I was born out here. I won't get lost, and El Cobre will look out for me." Without waiting for further objections, she loped off in the direction where Ellis had last seen Joanna and in which Angus had headed. With any luck, she'd find her. At least, she hoped so. Without Joanna, even in the black mood she'd been in lately, there would be no one to talk to, to laugh with. "Let her be all right," she prayed as she rode. "Please let her."

But several hours later, when Angus joined her, she had found no trace of her friend and was frankly worried. "I've looked everywhere," she said. "Now it's nearly evening, and if she's hurt. . . ." She broke off, seeing his face.

"I'll find her," he said grimly, shutting off a vision of Joanna, bloody and broken and beyond help. "I'll find her, if I have to sift every grain of sand and stinking cactus in this blasted place. But you should go back. Tino's about two miles west. You'll spot him from that ridge." He pointed.

"You're sure?" She felt sorry for him, sitting there as if he'd lost the most precious thing in the world and hadn't the least idea where to look for it. "I'll be glad to stay with you."

"You must be weary. Go on back."

She reached out and laid a hand over his, wanting to cheer him. "Joanna loves you very much," she said gently. "And I'm sure she's all right."

He wasn't about to reveal his anguish to this young girl, even though her words sent his blood surging. "And how would you be knowing?" he asked.

Francesca smiled. "Because she told me. And she'll be fine, because I like happy endings." She took up her reins and trotted off, leaving him elated and despairing both at once.

He rode in a wide circle, narrowing in toward the center, and once or twice he called her name: "Joanna." No answer came, only the echo of his voice.

The sun seemed caught on the peaks of the mountains, suspended in its descent and sending long rays of light across the plain. Dust motes danced, and each bush, rock, and tree cast its image in a dense shadow.

In one of those shadows he found her, hardly visible, face down, one hand stretched out as if she had been reaching toward him. For a moment he sat, too frightened to move, knowing that, if she were dead, a part of him had died with her, and that he would live out his life as one of these same, long shadows instead of the man he had hoped to be. Slowly he dismounted, knelt beside her, took hold of her small hand, and felt its warmth, the faint pulse.

Alive! She was alive! He turned her gently, saw her face, white under her tan. "Lass," he called, "lass."

With an effort, Joanna opened her eyes. They felt weighted by the pain and relief. "I knew you'd come," she whispered.

"Are you hurt bad?"

She rolled her head from side to side and winced. "I . . . walked this far." Talking was hard. Her tongue felt twice its normal size and rough as sandpaper. "Water," she said.

He went for his canteen, then knelt beside her again. "Can you sit, if I help?"

"Mmmm."

He took that as assent and slid an arm beneath her shoulders. So small she was! It was only her determination that made her seem big. Only the courage that he'd seen

159

shining out of her eyes.

She leaned against him, and he held the canteen to her lips. "Slowly," he warned. "No hurry now. I've found you."

She sipped. The water was precious, sweet as summer rain. Then she gave him a half smile, all she could manage. "I'm so glad," she said.

Chapter Twenty-Three

The chuck wagon was no ambulance. No matter how carefully Tino drove, it jounced and bumped and rocked Joanna where she lay on a bed of layered blankets. In spite of her protests, they were taking her to Francesca's aunt in Tucson. "And to a doctor," Angus had said. "I'll not be losing you, after the trouble I had finding you." His eyes twinkled, giving the lie to the rough statement.

"It'll be a week before we round up all the strays," the Colonel put in. "By that time, you'll be well enough to continue."

And all because of a stand of cholla, she thought. Because of a *plant!* And heaven only knew what else was in store for them on the long trail. But she had to go on. For Angus, for herself, for these men who, though they'd deceived her, obviously cared what happened to her. For the time being she was contented by their concern and the overwhelming relief that she was safe. However, although she tried not to think about it, images of her ordeal kept intruding — her helplessness as she staggered through the eerie silence of the desert, her thirst, the certainty of death like a deep abyss waiting to engulf her. Except for Angus, she could still be out there, decomposing under a bush with nary an indication of who or what she had been. She shuddered. Compared to death, the rest of what had happened was trivial. Alex was gone, and she had been spared for a reason unknown to her. Alex was gone, but his child lived. And regardless of what their marriage had been, she owed that child a proper home, a decent upbringing.

She squared her shoulders under the blankets. *When the drive is over, when I'm home again, I'll see to it,* she thought. *And never mind who says what or why.*

In spite of physical discomfort, the bouncing wagon, and the noisy Italian cursing of Tino, she closed her eyes and slept.

Angus, who had been at her side all along, leaned over and lightly smoothed her hair.

"Any nausea? Dizziness?" The doctor bent over her, lifting her eyelids and peering into her eyes as if he expected to see her answers written there.

"No. Not any more." She wished he'd go away and take his tobacco-stained mustache with him.

"But you did have?"

"When it happened, yes."

"You're lucky. You might have cracked your skull. Happens all the time. Horses are dangerous, and women should stay home where they belong."

The old goat! Lecturing her on manners and morals! She propped herself on her elbows. "How soon can I get up?"

"Not listening, are you?"

"No," she said shortly. "How soon?"

"A week. And, then, I'm not responsible for what might happen if you go on with this foolishness."

She'd be damned if she'd lie here that long, even if the bed was comfortable and Felice, Francesca's aunt, coddled her as though she was a child. Time was money. In a week they should be up on the Gila.

"Thank you for the advice," she said.

He picked up his bag. "Don't thank me, thank the Lord. He looks out for fools."

"Then he must have a full time job," she retorted, and

closed her eyes so he'd get the hint and leave.

He paused, his hand on the door. "Bull-headed," he pronounced, "like all women."

"And proud of it!" she snapped. "Good day, Doctor."

The door closed behind him, and she studied the sky beyond her window — blue sky, and against it a chinaberry tree covered with brilliant yellow berries. *Like a Christmas tree,* she thought and then realized that, indeed, it was almost Christmas. She had forgotten in the rush of the drive. And already she was restless, unused to sleeping late, having her meals served to her. Her internal clock had become that of the trail. Carefully she threw back the covers and got out of bed. The tile floor was cold on her bare feet, but she went to the window and peered out into the courtyard. Two sides of it were taken up by the Sandoval Dry Goods Store, the other sides belonging to house and kitchen where even now Felice Sandoval was busy supervising the preparation of the holiday *tamales, posole,* and Christmas lamb, and probably instructing Francesca on the rules of running a house and business.

The men had gone back to help round up stray cattle, Angus unwillingly. He hadn't wanted to leave her, and his last words to her had echoed her own sentiments. "Get well, lass. The world's a dark place without you."

She would, and without help from the doctor. Slowly she paced the room, alert for any return of the symptoms. She was scratched and bruised, and one hip ached dully, irritating but not serious. There was no sign of the earlier dizziness, and only a slight throbbing above one ear. Good! In spite of the luxury of the place and Felice's concern, in spite of Christmas and a lack of celebration, she'd be out of here in a few days, back where she belonged.

Funny how rapidly she'd gotten used to being away from civilization. Funny, and yet how lovely it was to be able to see a hundred miles, to hear the whistle of the unobstructed wind, to talk only of things that mattered instead of spending days in idle chatter and gossip. And what mattered? She stopped pacing and leaned her elbows on the window sill. Life — Angus — Allegra — the home place with horses in the pasture and fat cattle ready for market. Love and laughter. She'd lost sight of all those things somehow. But never again. She'd stumbled, carrying the burdens of everyone else's dreams, but now she had one of her own.

Gaspar Sandoval's Dry Goods Store was a cave filled with treasures. Joanna bought combs for everyone on Francesca's advice, a new hat for herself, and some rosewater for her complexion, a horsehair hatband for John, and then she lingered, looking for a gift for Angus. There was so much to see, to choose from! Saddles, bridles, bits, bolts of calico, wool, watered silks, and lush velvets, hats, boots, and shoes of all shapes and sizes, and in one room piles of Indian rugs and blankets, their brilliance like a shout in the dim light.

"When I come back, I'll want lots of these for my house," she said to Gaspar who was watching her with fascination.

She was so different from other ladies he'd known. Certainly beautiful, but as sure of herself as a man, direct in her speech without any of the flirtatiousness he was used to and enjoyed. Less than a week ago they had carried her into his house, and, now, here she was, striding through his store as if no accident had happened, her boot heels striking the wooden floor like castanets, knowing what she wanted as soon as she saw it without hesitation.

"They are always here, *señora*," he said, fingering the wool and automatically measuring the tightness of the weave, the thickness, while deciding whether or not to satisfy his very real curiosity. Finally, he cocked his head and spoke. "If I may ask, *señora*, why do you do this thing? Take cattle to California, when there are places closer that must also have meat?"

All her trading instincts were alerted. She sat down on the pile of rugs and explained, then asked a question of her own. "The territory is filled with cattle ranches. If we all sold locally, we'd ruin the market, and the price would fall. Don't you think?"

He considered. "Perhaps. Perhaps not. The country is growing. Every day more people come, and they must eat. This town . . . in twenty years . . . you will not recognize it. Or Phoenix. Or many others. I know this, *señora*. I have watched it happen."

Of course, he had. His family had been traders since the first Sandoval had headed down the Camino Real to Mexico, driving a flock of sheep and returning with iron, cotton socks, *bultos* of linen. Now here was this woman following on a similar trail. She would come back with money to spend and more cattle to sell.

Sitting there, she saw into his eyes. Markets were where you found them, and California was only one. With careful planning, they could open their own packing plants throughout the territory, as well as in San Diego. That way even the local ranchers would be selling to them.

"You've given me a fine idea," she said slowly. "I thank you. And I thank you and your wife for taking me in, taking care of me."

He bowed. "*De nada, señora.* We were pleased to help friends of *Señor* Harrington. He is family, as you know."

She nodded, then looked around the little room. "And I still need another present. A special one."

"For your *novio?*"

"For my friend," she corrected.

He went to a chest in one corner and took out a pair of fringed leather gauntlets. They were soft, supple, beautifully embroidered with beadwork.

Regardless of cost, she wanted them. "Perfect!"

Gaspar nodded to himself. Whether or not she admitted it, she was buying a gift for the young man who had brought her here, the man who loved her. Time would see to their differences, if such there were. He, Gaspar Sandoval, knew this also.

In a storm of protest, Joanna left the Sandoval house several days before Christmas. Francesca had tears in her eyes as she hugged her friend.

"*Vaya con Dios,*" she whispered in Joanna's ear. "Keep safe, and keep John safe for me." She had wished they could have Christmas together, but consoled herself with the hope that by next December John would be hers. All thanks to Joanna who had master-minded the plot, and whose accident, though dreadful, had kept both John and Angus coming to the house to see how she was.

Felice handed John, who was waiting at the door, a huge package of *tamales*. "For Christmas dinner," she told him, and began reciting the steps involved in cooking them.

John wasn't listening. He was watching Francesca, hoping to have a moment alone with her. The older woman, seeing his attention wander, chuckled. "Never mind. Eat them and enjoy. And now say good bye to Francesca. You can use the front parlor, but only for a minute." And as he stared at her, hardly believing his luck, she gave him a push. "Go! Leave the *tamales* with Joanna. Time is short!"

Francesca led him into the room, her skirt swishing, her small feet dancing, blessing her aunt for her insight. Once inside, she turned and looked up at him, adoration shining out of her eyes.

"I'll miss you," she said without preamble.

"Me, too." Even to himself he sounded like a dolt — and felt like one, alone with this lovely woman and unable to utter an intelligent word. "I mean . . . I'll miss you, too. But I'll be back before spring."

She moved closer, tilting up her face. "You won't forget?"

He shook his head, then succumbed to temptation and kissed her.

She had waited so long, dreamed of this moment. She put her arms around him and pulled him closer. The silly man! Did he think she'd break? But then, that was why she loved him — for his shy perplexity, his good manners. Except she didn't care a fig for good manners at this point. What mattered was the warmth of his mouth, the promise of passion scarcely held in check. She opened her lips and kissed harder.

"Are you certain you're up to this?" Angus asked as he walked into the room, having seen to the horses. He still had his doubts about Joanna's strength. She looked fragile, he thought, the bruises on her cheeks still faintly visible.

"I feel wonderful."

"All right. If you say so. Where's John?"

"Saying good bye to Francesca, and don't you dare interfere." She giggled. "John doesn't know what hit him."

"And probably never will."

"Is that a nice thing to say about your brother?"

"It's the truth. And well you know it. Did the two of you women sit up at night plotting?"

She giggled again. "Sort of. It worked, didn't it?"

"Aye." And had they plotted about him, too? They still hadn't had time to speak of the troubles between them, and the fact rankled. He wanted her back, wanted her friendship,

167

the closeness they'd had for such a brief time. And damn John! His farewell was going on too long.

"John!" he roared, and was faintly amused by the startled looks of the women. "We'll be leaving without you!"

Inside, John stepped away from Francesca with reluctance.

She drew a deep breath, then said: "I love you, John McLeod. And I'll wait for you like I've waited all this time."

He blinked. "For me?"

"Yes. Since the first day I saw you. I know I'm not supposed to be saying this, but I'm tired of playing games, sitting alone, telling myself stories about you and me. It's not enough. Not any more. It never was. But what happens next is up to you."

He kissed her again. It was so much more satisfying than speech, and her lips were so filled with promise.

"I'll speak to your father," he said, when he lifted his head.

Whether her father approved or not made no difference, but she lowered her eyes and tried to look demure. "Yes," she said. "Yes, please."

Chapter Twenty-Four

They were camped on the Gila River in the shadows of ancient ruins, a crumbling city in the midst of a sandy plain. After supper, Joanna wandered into the long-deserted town and looked in awe at the remains of houses and narrow streets, the earth tramped down by vanished inhabitants, those who had lived here and then disappeared. Tumbleweeds skittered through the open doorways of roofless houses, rose into the air as if on wings, and the scent of the creosote bushes was sharp and pungent, slicing through the dust raised by hoofs and the steady rush of a southwest wind.

Who were these people? she wondered. *Where had they gone? Here again was Angus's history. Here, rising out of earth and slowly melting back into it, was a record of a culture, remains to be marveled at and remembered — houses, walls, a great temple, dark against a sky glowing crimson and the orange of tiger lilies.*

In the distance she heard them — cranes coming home to roost — and, looking up, saw the glint of sun on outstretched wings. Their music was the music of trumpets, or, perhaps, the voices of those lost people, mourning for their home. She held to herself lest she crack open with the magic, lest somehow she rise up and follow, disappearing into sky as the vanished race had disappeared, with only her tracks in the sand to show that she, too, had come this way.

Unwilling to let her out of his sight, Angus had followed her and stood watching, touched by the ecstasy on her face that was lifted to the sky. Once before he had decided she was fey, blessed with the second sight, an inner ear that picked up voices others could not hear. Now, although he was aware of the haunting and mystical crying of the birds, he recognized that to her it was different, that in her heart she was one with them, in tune with the languages of the earth, and, therefore, possessed of insights that others, including himself, had not. He loved her the more for it, but he had not had a chance to tell her so, to speak his mind since they left Tucson. Slowly he walked toward her and was relieved when she saw him and smiled a welcome.

"Come and sit with me," she said, "and don't say anything for a minute. This place is magic. You'll see."

Words floated in his mouth like foam on a glass of ale, but he curbed them. If she wanted to be with him in silence, so be it. At least she wasn't giving orders, making decisions in that clipped way of hers that left no room for disobedience, as she'd just done over supper when the question had arisen whether to follow the river as it ran north, or to cut across the desert to Gila Bend, which meant a dry run of almost fifty miles.

While the rest of them had considered the pros and cons, she'd sat thinking. When she spoke, it was with that aura of command that he found so difficult to handle. "We'll make the dry run. It's stupid to go a hundred-some miles out of our way. We're headed west, let's stay headed west. The cattle can make it, and so can we. Frankly, I don't see the point of arguing about it." Then she'd walked away toward the ruins.

Deering looked after her, amused. "The lady has her mind made up. Ellis, what's your opinion?"

Ellis took the straw out of his mouth. "I think she's right, boss. Anything else's just a waste of time."

"And we're behind schedule as it is," the Colonel reminded them.

170

Angus got up, knowing they'd talk some more then bow to Joanna's dictate. "Let's just get on with it," he told them, then followed her.

Now, out of the corner of his eye, he studied her — the delicate profile, the determined chin. She'd changed since she'd been here, but so had they all. Circumstances had dictated the course of their lives, and he was the last one to find fault with her for that. But he'd be damned, if the two of them continued the way they had been — avoiding all contact, all serious discussion, and with that smooth-talking Harrington always at her heels, awaiting his own chance.

The birds had disappeared, swallowed up by sky. Now only the wind broke the silence, whistling through the ruins, moaning around the corners of the huge temple.

Angus cleared his throat. "I've come to speak my mind," he began. "And I'm sorry if I've intruded on you. But I cannot go on the way we have been."

In spite of herself, she smiled at the way his Scots burr became more pronounced the more agitated he became. "You're not intruding," she said. "And this is a good place to talk. Like being in a church or a holy place."

To hell with churches! That was just like her to lead him away from his purpose! "I've not got time for talk about churches, Jo. It's us we need to settle, beginning with me not telling you about the bairn. It was not my place to do so. And it was not in me to break your heart, your spirit, not when you were hanging on by the ends of your fingers, confused enough by the mare's nest you'd walked into."

She listened, soothed by his closeness, the soft blurring of his words, and what she perceived as a great honesty, a depth of character she'd never taken the time to analyze. She said: "I owe you an apology for that night. What Terrill said was so awful. And how he said it. Like we were all scum, you, me, ev-

171

erybody. I knew better, but I felt so alone. So foolish and lost. It was my husband he was talking about. It was my life, and I had a right to know. All I really wanted to do was crawl into a hole and die, but what I did was yell."

"Like a harpy." He quoted himself with a smile. "I did not think that's true, you know, even though you've done your best to make a believer out of me. It just seems we've drifted apart from the way we were, and I've had enough of your ordering me like I'm a servant, of havin' guilt on my head for what I did in good faith. I need to know where I stand, lass. I've loved you since the day we came in on the train, but I'll nae be wasting myself on a hopeless cause. You needn't answer now. God knows you've had enough to swallow. I'll be leaving you here in peace to think on it a while."

He got up and headed back the way he'd come. He'd done it — swallowed his pride and spoken the truth. The rest was up to her.

"Wait!"

This was how the French aristocrats had felt just before the blade descended, and Mary Queen of Scots going to the executioner mouthing prayers that couldn't numb the bite of the axe. He stopped, the muscles in his shoulders taut.

"Come back," she said. Then added: "Please, Angus."

He searched her face for a clue, but she gave him none.

How to begin! Francesca had talked about men and their pride, but she had had her share, too, and explanations came hard.

"I . . . ," she started, then stopped, warned by some deep-rooted instinct that this was her last chance, and that, if she loved him, she'd better make the most of it. He'd bared his soul, and, having done so, was, in his pride, quite capable of walking away, leaving her with nothing but the fading memory of a kiss.

"I'm sorry," she said, and then her words came out in a rush as if a dam had broken between her two selves. "I've bossed you, and scolded you, and turned into a harpy, like you said. I'm not sure why, but I have, and I don't like myself any more than you do. When you asked me that day if I'd missed you, I couldn't say it. Women aren't supposed to go around wearing their hearts on their breasts. It's stupid, but that's the way it is. I wanted to tell you that, when I got up and you weren't there, it seemed like the sun had gone out. That I was with people I didn't know, didn't want to know. But I was mad, and my pride got in the way. Pride always does, you know." She took a ragged breath and went on. "Ever since I got here, I've had to do things I never imagined doing. I had to change, and I did, but I lost something along the way. It's not your fault. It's mine. Can you understand that?"

He nodded, concealing his relief. "Aye, lass, but you cannot blame yerself. You did what you had to, like the rest of us."

"Yes," she agreed, "but I didn't have to lose myself to accomplish anything. I didn't have to accuse you about Micaela, when you were only thinking about me. What Alex and I had wasn't a marriage, but how could I know that? I was too naïve when I married him. I believed in him because I was supposed to. He wasn't a bad man, just a weak one who held onto me . . . or whoever else he could find . . . for his strength."

"Aye. And nearly doomed you in the process." He wished he'd met the hapless fellow. What wouldn't he have told him? But then, nothing could have happened between himself and Joanna. He'd have been forced to stand by and watch the man bring her down.

She shrugged. "It didn't happen. What did happen was that I held onto something that was never there to begin with.

I made up a picture and colored it the way I thought it should be, and I did you wrong because of it."

"I knew that. So I waited. I'm still waiting, come down to it. But I'm tired of not knowing where I stand. Of playing the fool, if you must know."

So he wanted her to say the words that couldn't be taken back, make the leap into the space between them that was as wide, as deep as an abyss. For a moment she wavered between truth and prevarication, but either way she was doomed. On the one hand to loneliness, on the other to a relationship with this man whom she loved but in many ways hardly knew. Would he, too, prove a disappointment — use her — and in the end betray her?

She looked hard into his eyes and saw the reflection of the western sky, saw herself, small, perched on a wall, the immensity of earth and the ruins of a lost tribe shimmering behind her. What was she without him but this frail being who was, at this moment, nothing but an empty silhouette? What was life but a series of risks?

He, too, had spoken of dreams but had the conviction to make them real, and never, not once, had he disappointed her, left her dangling without support. He had searched for her, when she was lost, and carried her to safety, and she suspected he always would.

She held out her arms, a gesture like the opening of wings. "Don't leave me," she whispered. "I don't think I want to live without you."

This was how he'd imagined it. Her in his arms where she belonged, with no misgivings, no false modesty, only the sweet warmth of her mouth, freely given, her body yielding to his demands.

"I'll nae be sleeping outside your door tonight, lass," he murmured. "Nor any night till we're in our graves."

She shivered. "Don't say that!"

"It's the truth, and I swear it. Dinna fash yourself about bad luck. We've both had enough of it to last."

They walked back slowly, reluctant to share themselves and their happiness with the rest, not noticing that the wind out of the west was rising.

"Looks like we're in for it." Ellis's words were muffled by the bandanna he'd pulled over his face. "The herd's gonna want to drift. And, Miz O'Keefe" — he turned to Joanna — "you'd better plan on sleepin' in the wagon tonight. No sense having that tent blown down on your head."

So much for best laid plans, she thought, and looked at Angus, amused.

Frustration was plain on his face, but he accepted the delay with a wry grin, then said: "Will you marry me in San Diego, lass, and keep my intentions honorable?"

There was no mistaking that he meant it, every word, and she knew that to the end of her life she'd remember this moment — the dust and sand blowing in their faces, the shriek of wind, the passion underlying his simply worded proposal.

"How many times do I have to say yes?" she asked, and her eyes sparkled even through the darkness of the storm.

Chapter Twenty-Five

The wind dropped at first light, and they moved out, only to be caught when it rose again, driving a whirling dust cloud that blotted out landmarks and pelted animals and riders alike with stinging particles that felt like hail. Instinctively the cattle attempted to turn away from the wind. Time and time again the herd, in one motion, swung around, stubbornly resisting the efforts of the riders to stop them. The pace was slow. They moved a mile, lost a half, moved again and repeated their actions.

To Joanna it seemed they were rotating inside a vicious whirlwind. She had lost all sense of direction and was unable to see, to hear, to breathe, even with her scarf tied across her face. If only the wind would stop! But it would never stop. They'd die in this maëlstrom, choke to death on the dust that caked in their mouths, clogged their noses, stung their eyes. And she had brought men and animals into this swirling hell.

There was nothing to do but go on, bent over in the saddle, taking the brunt of the storm head-on — the horse coughing, its head down, pushing against what seemed an impenetrable wall. On and on. Animals milling, raising more sand. Where was happiness now? In which direction was home? And then Joanna stopped thinking at all and clung to the saddle, her vision blurred.

By the time the wind dropped, in late afternoon, they were all unrecognizable, caked with dried sweat and the resulting mud. Horses and cattle stopped, shook themselves, and sniffed the ground in search of any grass that had, somehow, escaped the storm. Tino and the chuck wagon were nowhere in sight. As usual, he'd gone ahead of the rest, but now, in the faint visibility, there was no sign of him.

Frightened, Joanna looked at the others. "This could be trouble."

Deering stood up in his stirrups for a better look around. "We've got some daylight left, and we'd better use it. Henry, John, Angus, let's us get fresh horses and start searching."

"What about me?" Joanna wanted to know.

"You stay right here in case he shows up."

Ellis came in off the circle. "Looks like no chow tonight."

"Or sleep, either," she said. Their bedrolls and her tent were in the wagon as well as the food.

"You want me to go look, boss?" Ellis asked.

Deering shook his head. "Stay with the herd. We'll try to be back before dark."

Joanna dismounted wearily. No tent, no dinner, no Tino. Without him they were done for. "What if he's hurt?"

"We have to hope that isn't the case," Harrington said. "He might just have gotten turned around, and we wouldn't have seen him."

When they had gone, Joanna sat down on the ground and took a sip of water from her canteen, then realized that without Tino all the water they had was what each person carried. And now they were part way through a fifty-mile dry run.

"I guess we're in a real pickle," she said to Ellis.

"I been in worse."

She managed a smile. "Is that supposed to make me feel better?"

"Yes and no. You didn't think it would be easy, did you?"

"I'm not sure I thought at all, beyond getting to market."

He shifted in the saddle. "And speakin' of that, we're shy about twenty head. Must've got away when we couldn't see 'em."

And they'd never found thirty that had run off in the last stampede. Pretty soon they'd be down to none and the whole venture a loss. Joanna slammed her hands on her knees. "Why don't we just give them away? What's the use of this?"

Ellis realized that she was exhausted, her face covered with mud and grit, her eyes tinged with despair. "Don't take on," he said in another attempt to calm her. "We'll find them. And they'll find Tino, too. It's mighty hard to lose something as big as that wagon."

Slowly she got to her feet. "What can I do?"

"Nothin'. You just sit right there like they said."

Sit and do nothing. She found that intolerable, especially when there was trouble. "I wish I chewed," she said with a scowl, and he chuckled.

"No you don't. Mister Angus'd have himself a fit when your teeth turned brown."

In spite of herself she laughed, too. "You win that one. All right. I'll just stay here and chomp on my fingernails. Maybe get a fire built. You think it's safe?"

He glanced around. "Ain't much to burn up. Go ahead. That way they'll know where we are. Maybe even Tino'll find us."

Tired as she was, it was better to be doing something, keeping her thoughts at bay. On hands and knees, she scooped out a shallow pit, then got up and looked for some stones to put around it. Wood was harder to find. The creosote was sparse here, but she found several mesquites with broken branches and rotted stumps that she dragged back to the pit, and a few saguaro cactus ribs that might burn as well. Such a strange plant it was, she thought, tilting her head to look up at the giant that towered over her almost like a person with its stubby arms and crown of dried flowers. Distressed and weary as she was, she marveled at the peculiar things that clung to life — cactus, the cranes, the armadillos of Texas, even people. Most of all people, perhaps the most peculiar of all species, she thought wryly, each one different, yet similar in basic needs.

Perhaps someday she'd have the luxury of time to follow her thoughts to a conclusion, even keep a diary, a record of day-to-day happenings and her reactions. Something to pass on, as Angus had said. A guide book for their children and grandchildren. What would it be like to be back home and married to a man not Alex? Unbidden, the word came to her. *Paradise*. Life, even with its problems and pain, would be paradise with the right companion, the man whom destiny had appointed. The worst mistake she'd ever made had been marrying Alex. And why had she done it? She struggled to think back to the person she'd been. She'd felt sorry for him, she decided, and that was hardly a good reason. And he'd fastened on her, stolen her strength, and in the end betrayed her.

Angus was in all ways different. At the thought of him her body responded on its own with a small, hot flicker of hunger deep in her belly. That was one of the differences, she noted. Even in his absence he had the ability to ignite her response.

And she could stand here dawdling until dark, when she had a job to do. Time enough for foolishness when work was done, when the trail was a memory, when the men came back with Tino. She hoped nothing had happened to the little man — so sincere, so devoted to all of them, looking out for her in so many small ways. If it had, she, alone, was responsible for dragging them all on this mission.

She knelt by the pit, arranging twigs and branches, then reached for the matches she kept in her pocket. As she did, the other person who lived in her head, the stern taskmaster, the voice of reason spoke harshly. *You are responsible only for yourself*, it said. *What others do, they do because of who they are.*

"We're cursed. The lot of us. I should have put my foot down. Squashed this notion the first I heard of it. But you talked me into it, the two of you." John was missing Francesca, worried about Tino, and more tired than he'd ever been in his life. "This blasted country," he went on, without waiting for a response from Angus. "Look around! What d'you see, man? A cloud of dust. Cactus that look like Goliath. Others that jump out and grab you with hooks. We might as well be on the moon."

Angus heard an echo of his own despair of several weeks before. "It'll all come right. Nothing worth having is ever got easily."

"Bosh! Never mind your philosophy. Where d'you think he's got to?"

"He can't be far. The storm was too bad, and I doubt the mules would run off. More likely they found shelter and stopped dead, being mules."

"Aye. And where's shelter in this misbegotten desert?"

Angus searched what seemed to be a flat plain, knowing how tricky that level surface could be. A wash could be hidden anywhere, a small rise in the ground almost invisible, yet offering protection. To the north he saw mountains, cactus rising from rocky slopes, and below a crooked line of trees — ironwood, mesquite, the green branches of palo verde.

"Come on," he said, realizing that so many trees meant water, even if below the surface. "Let's ride over that way."

It was a narrow, crooked wash with steep banks, and they stopped at the edge, peering in both directions.

"I'll go one way, and you the other," John suggested. "If you find anything, fire a shot. I'll do the same."

The wind and blowing sand had obliterated all tracks. An-

180

gus rode slowly, alert for anything that would tell him that Tino had come this way. A raven croaked and took flight from a crooked branch of an ironwood, and overhead a hawk hovered motionless. Suddenly his horse stopped, snorted, stood with its head high, its ears pricked.

"What?" he asked it, knowing that anything strange might have attracted its attention.

The animal nickered once, and from around the bend came the unmistakable answer of a mule. The chuck wagon lay on its side, half in and half out of the wash. The mules, although tangled in harness, stood still, watching as he approached.

"Good boys," he called, hoping they wouldn't bolt and run off, dragging the wagon.

"*Signore.*"

He heard the weak call, then saw Tino, his leg pinned under the front wheel. Dismounting, he tethered his horse to a tree branch, then hurried to the little cook.

"Are you hurt?"

"My leg, *signore.*"

"Blast!" Angus knelt to assess the damage. Tino's leg was bent at an awkward angle beneath the wheel, and blood was slowly seeping into the sand under it.

"Lie still," he said. "I've got to unhitch these mules before they take it in their heads to drag the rest of the wagon over you. Hold on a wee bit longer. Is it bad?"

"Bad enough."

And he didn't dare fire a shot. Not yet.

Carefully he approached the near mule, unbuckled the harness, and retrieved one of the reins that had wrapped itself around a hind leg. "Good boy," he murmured in approval, blessing the intelligence of the animal. Most horses caught in the same situation would have thrashed themselves into a frenzy by now. He kept up a running stream of talk as he led first one and then the other out of the shafts and tied them securely near his own horse. Then he scrambled up the bank and fired a shot.

"John and the others will be here in a while," he said to Tino. "I cannot lift this by myself."

Tino nodded. "My fault. I think to get out of the wind, but the edge of the bank give way. I jump. But not far enough."

It was easy to visualize. "Dinna fash yourself." Angus knelt and offered Tino some water. "Accidents happen."

"But now there is no supper." Tino's face was wrinkled with pain and worry over the others.

"We've all gone without supper before," Angus said, touched by his concern and relieved to hear John coming up the wash at a careful lope.

He came to an abrupt halt, staring at the disaster. "God in heaven!"

"Never mind your curses. We've work to do. We've got to dig him out from under and then find the others."

Angus walked to the rear of the wagon and crawled in. He removed two lanterns from their hooks and handed them out to his brother. "Get these lit. The shovels are in here somewhere."

After a minute he found them in a pile against the side board. "Now we dig," he said. "And try to prop the wheel high enough to get him out."

They set to work without speaking, ignoring their own weariness, attacking the loose sand with determination. It was nearly dark when Angus put down his shovel. "Enough. I can pull him, if you steady the wheel."

Slowly, carefully, his arms around Tino's shoulders, he dragged him out and sat him against the opposite bank. The heavy wheel had ripped through his boot and gashed his leg.

Angus looked up. "Go for the rest of them," he said to John, hoping his horror at the sight didn't show. "I'll stay here and do what I can. And hurry, man. There's not time to waste."

Chapter Twenty-Six

The Colonel surveyed the scene in the wash — the wagon on its side, Tino leaning against the crumbling bank, the whole made eerie by the flickering lantern light — and took charge.

"I'll have to set that leg, and I'll need help. Joanna, see if you can't find the whiskey bottle. And if you have a petticoat and needle and thread in your box, we'll need those."

Obediently she hoisted herself into the wagon and searched for her box containing the clothes she'd brought to wear in San Diego and the small "housewife" of scissors, needles, pins, and thread. By a miracle, the bottle of whiskey wasn't broken, and she handed it out to Harrington. Further back she found her box and dragged it with her.

"Now what?" she asked.

"Now tear that petticoat up. I'm going to set this leg, and stitch the wound, then wrap it. I'll need your help, if you think you can handle it."

She remembered Allegra's birth. Handle it? "I can," she said.

"Good. I've already given him all the whiskey he can hold. The wound's nasty, but not as deep as we thought. Find the heaviest thread you have and bring it here." To Angus he said: "Hold his shoulders. I can't have him jumping around."

"He's passed out."

"Good. Let's hope he stays that way. Joanna, get me some light."

She brought the lantern and set it beside him, then went back for her petticoat. It was a good one, her best, but this

184

wasn't the time to mourn over an undergarment, not with Tino lying there, his face white and twisted. She gritted her teeth and ripped.

The break was clean, Harrington noted with relief. No crushed bone, no nasty splinters to pick out. Probably the man's heavy boot and the softness of the sand under the wheel had saved him from worse injury.

The squeak of bone as he pushed it together made Joanna jump. Without turning his head, he said: "Now, my dear, bring your needle and thread. Your hands are smaller than mine."

He wanted *her* to stitch the wound! To drive her needle through Tino's living flesh! "Dear God!" she gasped. "I'm not sure. . . ."

"Nonsense. You've done worse," came the stern reply. "Hurry now, while he's still out."

Her eyes sought Angus's and found encouragement in his level gaze, his slight smile. Swallowing hard, she knelt and peered at the wound, saw layers of muscle, fragile tissue, skin, clotted blood. "Pour some of that whiskey on this," she commanded. "Let's get it as clean as we can."

Then with great care she began to sew, drawing on all her skill as a needlewoman, on all the dreary hours she had spent as a child stitching her sampler. What were the words she'd labored over for so long? *Here my needle plies its task*. But never had she imagined a task such as this — the darkness, lit only by a single lantern, the wind gusting overhead, and before her the terrible fragility of the human body exposed and at her mercy. What kept her hands from trembling, her inner screaming from possessing her, she never, later, could remember.

When she had finished, when she had knotted the thread and snipped it with scissors, only then did she relinquish the

185

stern hold she had on herself. Burying her face in her hands, she wept.

With a curse — in the Gaelic, it was so much more satisfying — Angus laid Tino down and went to her. "Finish the rest," he said to Harrington. "The lass has had enough."

The Colonel, fashioning bandages and a rude splint, nodded. "She's an admirable woman. Make sure you treat her as she deserves." At that moment he'd have killed for his youth back, for the privilege of taking her in his own arms and giving comfort as Angus was doing. In his life he had had few regrets. He'd been lucky in that regard. Regrets only soured a man, made life intolerable. And he was one who had always enjoyed life to the fullest.

During the night the men worked in shifts, digging the sand out from under the high side of the wagon.

"Like Sisyphus," Harrington muttered, wiping sweat from his forehead. "The more we dig, the more comes down. We'll be at this for days."

"Except we don't have days," Deering reminded him.

"No need to tell me what I already know."

"And no sense wasting our breath on nonsense," John put in. Sisyphus! Who in hell was that? Sometimes his future father-in-law seemed out of place, like now in this ditch in the middle of nowhere, talking foolishness. And he still hadn't mentioned his plans for himself and Francesca. Time enough for that when they were out of here, back in some semblance of civilization, if such a place existed — which he was beginning to doubt.

Joanna lay in her bedroll beside Tino, both of them covered with quilts that had been pulled out of the wagon. Although exhausted, she slept fitfully, waking to watch the men

186

shoveling, to check on Tino who hadn't moved since before the operation.

Had she really done that? Stitched his ragged flesh together without fainting? The trembling of her body answered. She had, indeed. And then Angus had come to her, held her against him as she wept, his long, lean body somehow more comforting than softness, as if his strength leaked into her, giving her back her own. She wrapped her arms around herself to keep the feel of him, and, in spite of all that had happened, a smile softened the corners of her mouth. Love took so many guises, expressed itself in such different ways, most of which she'd never experienced. How strange it was, this link between a man and a woman. And how rare and precious to find it.

By morning the wagon was part way up, its side propped with branches hacked from nearby trees. Joanna built a fire and put the coffee pot on at the first sign of daylight, then went to check Tino.

He was awake and, though still ashen, was lucid and concerned about the rest, how they would eat, who would see to them.

"Don't worry," she assured him. "I can cook, and, if I don't know something, you can tell me."

"*Va bene.*" He closed his eyes, then opened them. "The *café*. For me, please, put in much sugar."

She laughed. "All you want, whenever you want. Just get better. We can't do without you."

He looked down at his leg, splinted and tied with her petticoat. "I am in your debt, *signora*. For what you did last night."

"You'd have done it for me."

"Of course."

"Then we'll say no more." She cocked her head at the sound of hoofs. "Here comes trouble."

"I pray not."

"Better pray hard then," she said.

Ellis rode in, still covered with the mud and dust of the day before, and dismounted with a groan. "Coffee sure smells good," he said, scrambling down the bank and surveying the wagon.

Joanna brought him a cup and stood listening as he recounted another problem. "Those twenty steers ended up on the reservation, and the Injuns won't give 'em back. I been arguin' with the head man, and he says what's there belongs to them. Wouldn't listen to reason. I figured he might listen to you better'n me."

"Hellfire!" Deering drained his cup and set it down. "If it's not Apaches, it's some other bunch. I'll go."

"I'll go with you," Joanna said.

"This is men's work," John snapped, and, as usual, found himself the object of an icy green stare from Joanna.

"The hell it is. Those cattle are ours, and no Indian's going to tell me otherwise. I'm going, and that's it." Joanna looked around for her hat, found it, and slammed it on her head, then went to find her shotgun.

Deering snorted. "I'll bet they regret it, when they're staring down that barrel."

"And see the look in her eye."

Angus thought she was a woman in a thousand, in a hundred thousand. After all she'd been through, she should have been prostrated. Instead, she appeared to have more energy than a swarm of bees. And she was his! And he wouldn't trade her for the crown jewels of Scotland.

Chapter Twenty-Seven

"People live here?" Joanna's voice rose in disbelief as she surveyed the squalid little settlement. "It's a disgrace."

"It's their choice," Deering said shortly. "They're not forced into squalor."

A few ragged children ran down the road after a scrawny dog. Other than that, the village seemed deserted, a cluster of *ramadas* and rough dwellings as insubstantial as the sand on which they sat.

"Those children look starved," she said, looking after them.

"And they could be farming, but they aren't. Don't bleed, Joanna, and don't go thinking our cattle can make a difference."

"Here comes the head cheese, and he ain't starving," Ellis said as the fattest person any of them had ever seen lumbered toward them.

He wore tattered trousers with a blanket around his torso, and his graying hair hung to his shoulders. Out of black eyes he regarded them with a look half mischief, half insolence.

"Why you come back here?" he said to Ellis.

Deering answered for him. "We've come for our cattle. Those over there." He pointed to a rough wooden pen where the twenty steers were milling aimlessly.

"They are ours." The man planted himself firmly, arms crossed over his massive chest.

"They are wearing our brands, and I have the papers to

prove it," Deering said, pulling the documents out of his pocket.

"White man's papers don't mean anything here."

With an effort, Deering kept his temper. "They'll mean something to your agent, especially when I tell him how you stole them."

The Indian curled his lip. "If you can find him. He's no good, either. For now, you're on our land. We didn't ask you here. But I am telling you to go." He stopped as an idea struck him, and, when he spoke again, it was with gleeful malice. "Maybe we make a deal. The woman for those cows. How about it?"

Joanna had heard enough. All her earlier compassion dried up, and in one swift move she raised her shotgun. "Ellis," she said, "go open that gate and get those steers moving."

"Yes, ma'am." He saluted the Indian with his own insolent gesture.

"You're a thief and a conniver," she went on, aiming at the huge belly. "And look how you live. Like hogs. Like trash. You should be ashamed."

His black eyes didn't waver. "Talk," he said. "Words mean nothing."

She'd have loved to pull the trigger, blow the ground from under his feet, and give him the scare of his life, but common sense held her back. "That's right. So you just stand there and keep your smart talk to yourself until we're out of here."

Where were the other people? she wondered. Surely this loathsome man wasn't the only inhabitant of the village. But no one came out to protest as the cattle filed slowly down the trail. In the whole place nothing moved except a tumbleweed bouncing aimlessly at the whim of the wind.

When she judged that Ellis and Deering had a decent start,

she locked eyes with the Indian. "All right," she said. "Turn around slowly and go back wherever you came from. And don't think we'll let you steal anything else of ours, because we'll be watching."

He obeyed, but not before a last insult. "Like all white people, you play tricks. I see now you are a man who wears women's clothes. Not worth one cow, even."

She opened her mouth, then closed it, refusing to be led into a response that would only infuriate her further. Obviously, that's what he wanted, this creature who resembled a washtub, who'd somehow managed, in spite of his bulk, to pen up her property and then refuse to return it. Deering was right. A thief was a thief, regardless of race.

"Son-of-a-bitch," she muttered. "And I was worried about the children."

When he disappeared through an open door in one of the houses, she turned and rode after the others, still cursing under her breath.

Chapter Twenty-Eight

Joanna was driving the chuck wagon with Tino lying cramped inside, and neither she nor the boys pushing the herd was wasting any time. Already they'd lost a day, and the dry run that had seemed feasible was becoming a desperate push toward water at the Gila. One of the barrels had broken when the wagon overturned, and there was scarcely enough left for coffee or to fill canteens. The animals were showing the lack, dragging their feet, bawling until she thought she'd have to cover her ears to get any peace. Water. Out here everything came down to water, or the lack of it. The wagon bumped and swayed, and Tino called out.

"*Signora,* you drive like a Roman, but this not a chariot."

"Sorry," she said over her shoulder, knowing from experience how he felt. "Are you in pain?"

"*Non c'é male.*"

"What's that mean?"

Tino craned his neck so he could see her. "It means not too bad."

"Good. Hang on." She swung them around a boulder that jutted out of the sand, then grinned. "Is this enough of the adventure you wanted?"

He looked out the front of the wagon and the brightness of the sky, then down at himself, his leg held together with the branches of trees and a petticoat, and thought of the miles he had wandered, the strangeness of them and of the people he'd met. "I think, yes," he said, then he allowed himself the luxury of daydreaming. It was always the same dream. In his

192

money box was the salary he'd saved for the last three years. Enough to buy a place of his own, a little *trattoria* where he could cook what he liked, what he knew best — rich sauces, pasta, fish from the sea, lamb raised on the fragrant herbs and grasses of the desert and tasting as it should.

"I think, *signora,* when we reach California, I will stay," he said.

She was startled. "You can't! We love you."

"Ah." His sigh was musical. "It is your life, not mine. For me, I want now to stay in one place. Maybe . . ." — he licked his lips that were dry and cracked — "maybe find a woman of my own."

It always came to that — the desire for another, an end to loneliness. She nodded to herself in understanding. For these men, these cowboys, there was only work and their own rough camaraderie to fill in the empty spaces.

"What will you do?" she asked.

"I think to buy a *trattoria.* You will come, and I will make a feast for you. Many good things . . . lasagna, *capretto,* fish right out of the sea. And wine. Water. . . ."

"Don't talk about water," she said. "It makes it worse."

"*Si.* How far now, do you think?"

"Beats me." She strained to see ahead, searching for the sight of the river as it made its big bend and headed west, but all she saw was the pale flatness of the desert, the scattered, naked trees, like line drawings against the sky.

She passed him her canteen, almost empty, but containing enough to ease his discomfort. "Here. Take it."

He had been thirsty before, many times. "No, *signora.* It is yours."

"Don't be so stubborn. You're the one with the broken leg, and, if you get a fever, we mightn't be able to help. Just drink it!"

She was a sensible woman, and strong. Just see how she handled the mules! And rightly, if he were to become ill, he would only be a further burden. *"Grazie,"* he murmured to her, and then went back to his dream. A woman like her would be hard, indeed, to find.

Rupert raised his great, horned head. He was an old steer and wise. He had led many drives, east and west, and he understood, in the dark channels of instinct, exactly how water smelled. Sweet. Sweeter than the greenest grass. Behind him the others followed suit, slowing their steady pace, raising their heads to catch the far-off scent. And then they sighed, a moan like air rushing out of a bellows, a collective thanks for an end to thirst. As one, they began to run in a straight line for the river. No one made an attempt to hold them. They would stop on their own, wade into the shallows, and drink and cool their feet like tired children.

They passed the wagon in a flat-out race, splitting apart in two huge wedges. The mules pricked up their ears and began to move faster, and Joanna braced herself, using all her strength to hold them.

The bumping jolted Tino out of his illusions. "What?" he cried out. "What?"

"The river!" she called back. "Hang on tight!"

Content, the herd spread out along the bank where the grass was plentiful.

"We ought to lay over a couple days," Deering said, looking out at the grazing cattle. "Anybody think otherwise?"

No one dissented, and Joanna was relieved. Maybe she'd get a chance at a bath, if the water wasn't too cold. Upstream about half a mile, she'd discovered a small inlet screened by trees that was perfect for privacy and bathing. At the very least, she'd get the caked dust off herself and out from under what fingernails she still possessed. A glance at the men told her what she must look like — haggard, filthy, every seam and wrinkle ingrained with dirt — hardly a vision to entice a lover.

"That being the case, I'll go hunting tomorrow," the Colonel said. "This country's full of quail, and I, for one, could use a change of diet."

Tino looked up, his eyes bright. "*Uccellini*. You shoot, I cook."

"No. *I* cook, and you tell me how," Joanna corrected him, then looked puzzled. "What was that you said?"

"*Uccellini*. Little birds. In Italia is special dish."

"Before I cook anything, I'm going to take a bath," she said. "After that, you can give me a lesson. And, now, I'm going to scrub the dishes."

"I'll help you." Angus had been watching her and realized she was running on sheer nerve. So were they all, he supposed, but it had to be worse for her, barely recovered from a concussion and in no way used to the strenuousness of the trail.

She looked up at him, grateful. "Thanks. I won't say no."

"And if you did, I'd help anyhow. It's not an easy task, what we're doing."

"It sounded easy, though, didn't it? Like that Indian told me . . . 'words mean nothing.' Maybe he was right."

She picked up a bucket and headed for the river, and he took it from her. "I'll do the carrying. You come along for the walk. And as for words having no meaning, there's two sides to that like everything else. Are the words I love you only gibberish, or do you understand?"

Her body responded before her brain, the hot coal of desire she carried deep in her belly igniting, radiating through her. Whether meaningful or not, language was a powerful tool she thought in that brief second before he put down the bucket, opened his arms, and she went into them, into that place where no words were needed at all.

Across the river, high on the opposite bank and hidden by a thick stand of trees, Terrill watched and was consumed by the flames of his own desires and a searing hatred that rose in him and tasted like hot iron.

Chapter Twenty-Nine

"Go on, all of you. Bring back lots of birds, and don't worry about me." Joanna flapped her arms and shooed the men out of camp. "I'm going to take a bath and be lazy till you come back."

"And you've earned it," Harrington said.

"We've all earned it. Even the animals."

Humming under her breath, she collected a towel, a piece of rough soap, and a change of clothes, then set off upriver. The day was warm, although it was January and nights were still below freezing. The river was bound to be cold, but no matter what, she intended to get clean.

It was a pleasant walk, with the river gurgling at her left, and on her right cattle grazing or simply resting, absorbing the warmth of the sun. Scotty and Chapo rode slowly among them, ever alert for trouble, although trouble seemed far away on such a morning. From somewhere came the scent of flowers, as if there were blossoms in hidden places, and around her a few bees buzzed, their small bodies like golden darts in the sun.

The river made a slight curve. She was out of sight of camp now, nearly at the little cove she'd found the day before, an ideal spot, with sand running to the water's edge. She sat down and pulled off her boots and socks, then tested the water. It was icy, but she was determined. Quickly she pulled off her riding skirt and flannel shirt, the long johns that seemed to be growing to her skin. "Here goes!" she said to herself, chuckling, and waded in.

The bottom was stony under her bare feet, the current

rounding the bend swift. With a gasp she lost her balance and fell, surfaced with her arms flailing. It wasn't so bad once she was used to it — once she was numb all over, she thought with a grin. But she'd lost the precious piece of soap when she'd gone under. Well, she'd have to make do with a good scrubbing, sticking her head under to get rid of the sand embedded in her scalp. And do it fast before she froze.

As she headed for shore, she blinked water from her eyes, then reached for her hair and wrung it out. Once on firm ground, she grabbed the towel and wiped her face, then wrapped it around herself. Heaven! It was heaven to be clean again!

And then she saw the man who stood watching, the look on his face that of an animal stalking its prey. Staring into his eyes, she realized that he was an animal, that behind the visible lust was a person without conscience, a man who would kill her without regret or remorse. But before that he'd use her and take pleasure in doing it.

As the Colonel predicted, the hunting was good. In a few hours they had brought down enough birds to feed everyone, although Angus had hated the process. Deer were one thing, the small, top-knotted quail another. After the first few rounds, he'd held his fire and let the others have their sport.

Riding a little apart, he saw two horses picketed in the brush and out of curiosity went to investigate. Immediately he recognized them and swore under his breath. So that no-good Fox was out here, spying, probably intending to make off with a few head or stir up trouble. He soon found the remains of a fire, but no sign of Terrill. Cautiously he circled the little campsite, then headed back to the others, worry gnawing at him.

"His kind keep turning up till they're planted six feet under," Deering said, when he heard. "But he's around some place, and on foot. Let's have us a real hunt, instead of picking off tame birds." Already his eyes gleamed with the possibility of a chase.

John sighed, his desire to have a talk with Harrington thwarted again. "He's a bad penny, no doubt of it, but we'd better find out why he's out here before we do anything. He's done nothing to us, after all."

"Yet," Deering shot back. "Nor will he, if I find him."

"Let's spread out. Take a look at the trail on this side of the river at the same time," Harrington suggested.

Angus couldn't squelch a growing uneasiness. Joanna had mentioned a bath. She'd be alone and unarmed. "I'm going back to camp."

Harrington glanced at him, alert. "You don't think . . . ?"

"I don't know what I'm thinking, but Joanna's alone."

"I'll go with you."

They had reached the crossing when two shots rang out.

No one would hear her scream or come to her aid. She had only herself and her wits, such as they were, and the pistol in the pocket of her skirt, if she could get to it, if he hadn't searched her things and found it.

Joanna said: "What are you doing here?" — and even to her she sounded frightened, like a rabbit just before its death throes.

"Watching you," he said, and took a step toward her.

"Keep away."

"No." He shook his head slowly. "No."

She whirled and ran, but the stones were sharp, and he caught her easily, brought her down hard on the ground and held her there, her face in the dirt.

"You don't want to run," he said. "It's not right." He ran a rough hand down her back, cupped her buttocks, and laughed a laugh that was almost a whimper. "Why'd you do it? Why'd you leave me? I never done anything to you."

She had never known insanity, but recognized it in his voice, his hand crawling over her flesh. And she was helpless, pinned down, every muscle in her body clenched in terror, awaiting the moment when he'd be on her, in her, whatever way he chose.

"You shouldn't have. And you shouldn't have let those men touch you. I knew about it. All along I knew, but you thought you were so smart. You thought I didn't see, but I did, and it made me sick. Real sick, Mama, down in the bad place."

Joanna's eyes shot open. Had he called her *Mama?* She was certain he had. And now she was certain he was mad, gone over the edge to some place where everything was twisted, where one person was indistinguishable from another, and revenge was all that mattered. The sudden insight gave her courage. She drew a breath, a slight one, and took a desperate chance. "Now, Son, you just had a bad dream. Not to worry. When you wake up, you'll see how it is." Then she prayed.

His hand stopped its searching and squeezed her until she almost cried out. "Don't lie to me," he whispered. "Not ever. You're coming with me this time, and I'll never let you go. Nobody's gonna touch you, except me."

He grabbed her hair and lifted her head, and she saw again that horrifying nothingness behind his eyes, as if he were already dead and determined to take her with him.

Keeping her face still, she said: "If I'm going with you, I'll need my clothes. It's not decent going without clothes. You know that, don't you, Son? You know how the devil works, how he calls up evil even in people like us."

Terrill frowned. "Evil? There's no evil. Why'd you have to say that?"

"Because your mama knows. And you love your mama. You listen to her." Had she said the right thing? She waited, the pounding of her heart threatening to choke her.

He was bewildered. She read confusion in his face, in the touch of his hand. She said: "I can't ride out of here naked. They'll all see. All the others. You'll shame me, Terrill, shame your own mama, and they'll laugh at you. Yes, they will."

One hand clenched her skin, the other yanked her head further back. "I'll kill them. Just like I killed him with his fancy ways. It was easy . . . like pickin' off a rabbit. He shouldn't have touched Micaela. It was wrong. And now she's dead, too. Everybody's dead. That's what happens to whores."

Comprehension, then rage, poured over her like a wave, pounding in her head, shutting off speech. He meant Alex! He'd murdered her husband and then gone on the same as always, sliding around among them like a snake full of venom and hatred, and none of them knowing. She wanted to scratch out his eyes, crack his head open, and trample his brains into the dirt. On that long-ago afternoon, standing by Alex's grave, she had vowed revenge, and, by God, she was going to have it. Somehow she'd get out from under this creature's vile hands, somehow he'd pay for what he'd done, and never mind the threat to herself.

She whispered: "Alex." It came out a hoarse croak.

He laughed without humor and brought his face down close to hers. "Don't play the grievin' widow. You're a whore, same as the rest. I seen you last night with the brother, and I seen that Harrington always on your tail. Now, it's my turn."

He smelled like the varmint he was, as if his evil gave off a

201

stench. She pulled away from him as far as she could. "I'll see you in hell," she said through her teeth.

"Shut up." He yanked her hair hard, then slid his hand around her throat.

Hatred, fear, gave her strength. "Let me go," she ordered. "Let me go now."

For some reason she didn't understand, he sat back on his haunches, staring at her. She forced herself to lie motionless, every muscle primed for flight. If only she could get to her pistol! But he was still too close to chance it.

He seemed to have gone into a trance, hypnotized by the sight of her, his face as blank as a stone. His silence was worse than his ravings, and the silence of the afternoon pressed down around them as if they were sealed off from the world, inside a glass jar, caught like insects, unable to move or escape.

When she could stand it no longer, Joanna pushed up on one hand, clutching the towel to her body with the other. It was a risk, but anything was better than lying helpless.

"Stay still!" He snapped back to consciousness.

"I'm cold."

"You don't know what it is to be cold."

He seemed normal now, and all the more dangerous. She licked her lips. "Can I get dressed?"

He curled his lip, and she remembered how she'd always hated that habit of his, that sneer, as if he had found them all beneath contempt. "Go ahead. Can't have you freezin' to death till I'm through with you. But don't try nothin'. I'll be right beside you."

She stood slowly, covering herself as best she could with the towel and realizing that she would have, at best, one chance and no more. Moving carefully, her skin crawling under his lustful gaze, she took her long johns off the rock and pulled on the bottoms. At least he hadn't touched her again. Modesty made her turn away to thrust head and arms through the top. To be seen by such a creature! It was almost worse than his hands on her. She shuddered, then caught herself. Emotion had no place here. He was a murderer, a rapist, and her only chance lay in using cold logic. Later she could give in — weep, scream, curse. If there was a later.

As calmly as she could she asked: "Where are you taking me?"

"You'll find out. Hurry it up."

She reached for her skirt, felt the heaviness in the pocket. The pistol was still there. All she had to do now was remove it. But how to distract him long enough to do it? "My boots," she said. "I need my boots. They're over there."

"Get 'em yourself."

"All right. I'm going." Holding the skirt at her side, she walked gingerly over the stones, then bent down as if to pick up her boots. Slowly, not daring to breathe, she reached deep into the skirt pocket. Her fingers curled around the pistol grip, and she remained bent over for a minute, feeling the weight of the weapon, judging the distance between them.

"Hurry up," he growled. "We ain't got all day."

With one smooth motion she pulled the gun and aimed it.

He knew she was a dead shot, and he could read her intentions in her eyes that had gone hard and steady. Killer eyes. He'd seen them before. The bitch! She'd tricked him, sweet-talked him, only to turn on him like all the rest. Like his mother, swinging from the rafters, her face swollen, turning blue. Like Micaela and that other one whose name he'd forgotten, but who'd started this trouble. He'd make her pay. Make her grovel. Then he'd have her, shoving a rag in her mouth so he couldn't hear her smart talk. With a roar, he lurched toward her across the small stretch of sand, his arms stretched out.

Her first shot caught him in the chest, but he hardly felt it. The second was lower down, a gigantic bubble exploding in his gut. One more step. One more and he'd have her, bring her down, teach her not to give herself away. And then there was only the pain, and the taste of his own blood, and the darkness that was unexpectedly sweet.

He fell at her feet, and she stood looking at him a long time. "That was for Alex," she said, her voice like a bell in the silence.

His eyes flickered open. They were filled with hate. He was still alive, watching her as if at any moment he'd get up and come at her again.

Deliberately she raised the pistol. "This one's for me," she said, and pulled the trigger.

Once again she took off her clothes and waded into the river. Maybe she'd never wash off the smell and feel of him, but she meant to try. And, when she had finished, she'd go back and tell the others. And Angus — what would he think of her now that she'd killed a man? Well, she wasn't about to lie or whitewash her actions. She'd done it — avenged Alex's death and saved herself, and she was glad.

"Lass." Angus put an arm around her waist, but she stepped away. Coddling was the last thing she wanted — or expressions of worry over her state of mind.

"I'm all right. He killed Alex, and he was going to kill me. After he raped me." She swallowed, fighting off the memory of Terrill's hand like a spider on her back. "He was crazy, and we never saw it. Maybe we were all too caught up in ourselves to notice. He was a killer on the loose and, if you think I'll not sleep at night, forget it. I'll sleep all the better, knowing he's not around. We'd better bury him, though. And check his pockets. Maybe there's somebody we should notify."

Deering cleared his throat and cocked an eyebrow at Angus who was fighting conflicting emotions. All this time he'd worried about what she'd do when she found out about what he'd done — and here she stood, firm on her feet, admitting she'd shot a man and had no regrets. Maybe he didn't know her at all, he thought in bewilderment.

A search of Terrill's pockets turned up a tobacco pouch and a few blood-stained bills.

"A loner," Deering said. "Probably his family was as glad to get rid of him as the rest of us."

Mama, Joanna recalled. "He . . . he thought I was his mother for a minute. She must have left him. I'm not sure. Everything was all mixed up in his head . . . me, Micaela, Alex . . . and he kept babbling and touching me until I couldn't stand it."

"Did he . . . did he hurt you, Jo?" Angus had to ask.

She shook her head, her lips quivering at the thought of what might have happened. "No. He never got the chance."

"Thank the Lord." He read the signs of collapse on her face and took her arm. "I'll take you back. No sense your having to watch the burial. There's a brave lass."

And she was brave, no doubt of it, the way the Scottish women he knew and had read about were brave. They'd fought beside their men, defended their homes with dirks, daggers, rusty arms, whatever came to hand. With a woman such as this, a man could be proud, could hold up his head because he'd won her, because he respected what she was, adored her for her loyalties and her courage.

"You're a warrior, lass," he said, boosting her into the saddle. "Dinna doubt it."

So he wasn't shocked. He didn't hate her. Relief swept through her and a hint of pride at his praise. Still, she wouldn't let him know what she felt. Some things were better kept to one's self. "I did what I set out to do," she said. "Now it's done. Now we can look to the future."

Chapter Thirty

The rain began as a fine drizzle, then intensified. Joanna lay awake, listening to it beat on the sides of the tent. You prayed for rain, but, when it came, it was either too late to do any good, or it fell in torrents and made life miserable. And she was miserable enough, haunted by a nightmare in which Terrill's head split open like a melon, leaving only the thin stem of his neck. This, in spite of her brave words to Angus. Every time she closed her eyes, she saw Terrill's face dissolving in slow motion — the pulp of his brains, the blood spurting out and coloring the sand. As a result, she was asleep on her feet, moving by rote, her senses dulled, wondering how long it would be before the image faded and she could rest undisturbed.

Since the shooting she had lain awake every night, coming out from her tent when the riders changed shifts for their company, or to listen to the sad Spanish melodies Chapo and Juan were so fond of singing to the herd. Somehow the two Mexican cowboys always knew when it was their turn to ride. No matter how soundly they slept, they were up and alert at the right time.

"How do you know?" Joanna asked Juan as he came to the fire for a quick cup of coffee before he took his turn. "You don't even have a watch."

Juan's eyes crinkled at the corners. He loved the *señora,* was proud of her — her way with horses, her politeness toward him, and, *Dios,* how she could shoot! He pointed to the sky. "*El reloj de los Yaquis, señora.* The stars tell me."

Of course. She should have figured it out for herself — the

Yaqui clock, the universal timepiece. And there was Orion the Hunter rising in the east, stalking through the shreds of storm clouds as he had done since the beginning of the world. For a reason she couldn't fathom, the notion gave her peace. Regardless of the actions of people, the earth turned, the stars stayed in place, the seasons followed in accepted pattern. What was she in the face of such rational magnificence? *A grain of mustard seed.* The Biblical words came back to her. And so were they all. She had killed a man who would have killed her, a murderer by his own admission. In all the splendor of space, worse things had happened, been absorbed, forgotten. The pendulum swung, the present became both past and future on the instant.

Angus came in and dismounted, nodding at Juan. "They're quiet tonight. You shouldn't have any trouble."

"Bueno." Juan downed his coffee, took his horse, and left, already humming to himself.

"Can't sleep, lass?"

"I think I can now."

"Why?"

She told him, fumbling to catch the thread of her thoughts, and, while they stood, the rain came hard, blowing into their faces.

"Turn the horse out and come inside," she said. "No sense getting any wetter."

She lit the lantern and waited while he took off his slicker. Then she said slowly: "It's possible that we don't count for much. That we move on our little paths, doing the best we can, and then life's over before we know it. Or, like you told me, it's also possible we can make history, leave a sign for others to follow. I killed a man who needed it, but I've been seeing it every time I close my eyes. And then I wondered what *you* saw and might be thinking about me. It frightened

208

me. All of it. I don't want to leave only a killing behind. The taking of life, even a bad one, isn't the same as giving life to someone, and, besides, I've been scared that I'd lose you . . . again. Does this make sense?"

He'd been listening, watching her expressive face in the yellow light, and his comprehension was swift. Hadn't he had the same doubts, suffered not so much from qualms of conscience as from the fear of what she would think of him?

"Aye, it does," he said, hunkering down beside her. "More than you know. When Mellen and I went after the missing horses, we shot the thieves . . . three of them . . . and left them lying there. That was his notion, not mine. But all the way back, I kept wondering how you'd take to the idea that I'd killed a man. And I didn't speak of it till now. But what I believe is that we're neither of us killers. We've done what we had to, and that's nae such a bad thing when you consider the alternative. This is a new country, and we're both strangers to its ways. Me more than you. There's those who come here in search of a better life, and those who come with no regard for life at all, not even their own. Over and over you've said you've changed, but so have we all, and who are we to judge ourselves when even good citizens call what we did justice?"

He wasn't given to long speeches, but this had been one of his longest, and every word spoken with a passion that suggested truth. She felt herself relaxing, falling into the sleep that had eluded her. Then she jerked awake.

"How did it happen? With the rustlers?"

"I followed Mellen. Thought he might be heading into trouble, and I was right. He found the thieves, but there was a third, skulking in the bushes, ready to shoot him in the back. I got there in time to prevent the murder of a good man."

"Did you dream of it?"

He traced her cheek with a gentle finger. "If you think

209

back, you'll remember that soon after that we had a fight and that wiped everything else out of my head. And then came the night with Terrill. So, no, I did not dream, or, if I did, it was about you, lass, and what I was going to say when I had the chance."

She leaned into his hand. "I keep seeing it over and over. I'm afraid to close my eyes for fear it'll start again."

"It'll not come tonight. Tonight I'll hold you and keep the bogies away." And that was all he'd do. Passion would have to wait until she was ready for him.

"I do love you," she whispered. "Very much."

He knew. She was the piece of him that had been missing, the shadow figure that had walked behind him all his life, tantalizing, never quite seen, only there — a chimera that beckoned him on, set his feet on roads he'd never thought to travel.

Curled up against him, she sighed once as if releasing evil. "I think when we get to San Diego I'd like to see the ocean," she said.

"It's a lovely but fearsome thing. I'll take you myself." He felt her relax still more. "We'll sit and look as long as you like."

"Is it blue?"

"Sometimes. And sometimes it's as green as your eyes."

His arms were around her, and his warmth. His voice was like a lullaby, sweet and soothing. In all her life she had been the one who gave comfort and strength, but now the situation was reversed. She moved closer.

"Angus?"

"What, lass."

"Thanks."

He didn't answer. Tilting her head to look at him, she saw he had fallen asleep. Oh, well, they'd said enough, found a common ground, erased many of their fears. And one day soon they'd be at the edge of the sea with the wind in their faces and the long road behind them.

Chapter Thirty-One

They passed Oatman Flat where Olive and Mary Ann Oatman had been captured by Apaches only forty years before. "Apaches." Deering, as usual, was eloquent on the subject of Indians. "Killed the family and took the girls, then sold them to the Mojaves as slaves. One died. The other had her face tattooed by the savages before she was rescued."

Violence! It seemed everywhere in this place. "What happened to her?" Joanna asked.

"Heard she married."

"And her face?"

"Reckon she lived with it, same as her husband."

And how did she feel, that woman marked for life? What fearful memories awakened her in the night? Her own nightmares had begun to fade, thanks to Angus. Mostly, she slept soundly, aware of his presence and grateful for it.

At Agua Caliente, they all bathed in the hot springs, and Joanna, accompanied by Tino who was hobbling on a rude crutch, bought provisions from the little store. Outside the Hotel Modeste the invalids, who had come to take advantage of the springs, sat in chairs and stared in wonder at the cavalcade of cattle, horses, men, and the lone woman, the picture of health, who strode about issuing orders and drove a team of mules as if she had been born to it.

"Poor devils," John said. "Sitting there waiting to die."

"Whatever we're facing, it's better than what they have to look forward to," Angus commented, and stepped up on his horse, never noticing that the eyes of one of them, a young girl, followed him as if she were seeing a vision.

From her seat on the wagon, Joanna watched, touched by the pathetic scene. There she'd been feeling sorry for herself, when she might have been here, among these scarecrows, with the girl whose life was running out, although she might not know it.

As she drove by, she waved and called out: "Good luck!"

The girl waved a listless hand, then let it drop back into her lap, as if even that small gesture was too much of an effort. All the way across the bare desert, Joanna kept seeing her — the pale, lank hair, the sunken eyes — and scolding herself. Life was hard, it was often cruel and merciless, but, as Angus said, it beat the alternative all to hell.

The rain began again as they made their way through the pass toward Yuma, but a watery sun leaked yellow light across the western horizon as they came down out of the mountains. Grass was non-existent on the desert floor. Only the ubiquitous creosote, the spidery branches of ocotillo, seemed to thrive.

"We better get 'crost that river quick," Ellis said, his face creased in a frown. "Even a bird couldn't find dinner here."

"It's not much better on the other side," Colonel Harrington informed him. "Won't be till we get to Warner's Ranch."

"*If* we get there."

"Where's your faith, man?"

Ellis looked behind him at the mountains. "Must've left it back there."

"Nonsense!" Harrington shouted. "Now I'm going to ride in and check on the river. See some old friends, and find out what I can."

Deering spit and asked: "Mind if I come along?"

"You're welcome to. I haven't seen Isaac Polhamus for

years, but he knows the Colorado upstream and down, and, if anybody can advise us, it's him."

"How's that?"

"He was one of the first steamboat pilots. Came here in the 'Fifties, when they found out the river was navigable up as far as Fort Mohave. And he's still at it, although the railroad's taken away a lot of his business."

"It's not done much for us lately, either."

"I've been thinking about that. Maybe it's time we changed the way we do business. Times change, and I'm not sure drives like this one are in the cards for the future."

"Christ, I hope not! I'm getting too old to do this every winter." Deering laughed, but the ache in his back seemed permanent. "Any chance of getting a bath?"

"Absolutely. Yuma's got everything . . . now," he added, remembering the first time he'd seen the little settlement with its mud and stick houses, its saloons, brothels, and one sad excuse for a hotel. "We'll get cleaned up, then pay a call on the captain."

Ellis watched the two ride off, before riding back to the herd. He'd seen the Mississippi, the Red, the Río Grande, but he had a hunch the Colorado was going to out-do them all.

The adobe house was large and imposing, and Deering whistled. "It's a mansion! Your friend's done well for himself."

"He earned it." Harrington knocked on the carved wooden door. "And he has a lovely wife. Sacramento. Fine woman. Doesn't speak much English, though."

The woman who answered his knock was dark-haired and dark-eyed, and she was lovely, Deering thought, especially with the welcoming smile she gave them.

214

"*Señor* Harrington! Come, come! It has been long time! Isaac, Isaac!"

Isaac Polhamus, white-haired and smoking a cigar, greeted them as heartily as his wife and led them into the parlor.

"Sit down and tell me what's happening. It's been . . . how long? Nine years, at least. I can't keep track of time any more. Goes by like the river. What brings you back?"

The Colonel and Deering settled in, enjoying the warmth of the fire and pulling out cigars of their own. When Harrington had his going, he leaned back with a sigh.

"Good to be in a house again, I might tell you. And on a chair, instead of the ground. We've been on the trail about two months, and it seems longer every day."

Polhamus looked at him, puzzled. "I thought you were through trailing cattle."

"So did I."

"The railroad," Deering put in. "A fine thing, if you can afford it. At the moment, we can't, so here we are on our way to California."

Polhamus nodded. "It's put steamboating nearly out of business. Mostly, I run excursions upriver these days. But that's progress, I guess, or what passes for it. California, eh? Why?"

When Harrington finished his explanation, the three sat in silence, each man with his own thoughts. Then Deering said: "So we have to get our cattle across the river, and the Gila's been on the rise with the rain. What are our chances?"

Years on the water had given Polhamus an almost intuitive knowledge of the river's whims. He was in tune with it — with its sounds, eddies, shoals, and the way it could change from placid to fearsome in an instant. Now he said: "The Colorado's rising, too. Nothing that can't be handled, if we think it out, and if we don't waste any time. Your best crossing is downstream, so you don't have to cross two rivers, and your problem will be the depth and the current. Unless a dam goes out somewhere, and then we'll all be in trouble," he added with a twinkle.

"So?" the Colonel prodded.

"So my idea is something we've done once before. Don't see why it won't work again. But the sooner the better, and that means tomorrow afternoon, at the latest."

"I've heard some mad schemes in my day, but this tops them all." John was pacing by the campfire, fighting his urge to throw in his hat and leave these people who thought to subdue the elements with boats and poles.

"It'll work. It has to," Joanna said. "Otherwise, we're stuck here."

"Or our cattle are drowned, and we're worse off than we were before." Angus had taken a long look at the river — its roiling, rust-colored water, the swift and deadly current — and it seemed more threatening than the ocean, or maybe he was turning into a desert rat, distrusting all but the shallowest puddle. Queer what this country did to a person, especially one accustomed to the burns and lochs of Scotland.

The plan was complicated but not without precedent, as Polhamus had stressed. He and Jack Mellon, another pilot, would take their steamboats, the *Mohave* and the *Gila*, and block the river downstream from the crossing with the help of local Indians in small boats, who would prod the frightened, swimming cattle out of danger and toward the far bank. Joanna, Tino, and the chuck wagon would be ferried across on one of the steamers.

"We'll take about two hundred fifty head at a time," Harrington said. "Give the first bunch a chance before starting

216

the second. Who wants to volunteer to lead off?"

The men looked at each other, hesitant, then Rain grinned. "Hell, I grew up along the Red, and I can swim as good as any of those Indians. I'll do it. Only I'll need a horse that's not scared of a heck of a lot of water."

"Nighthawk." Scotty offered his own horse without hesitation. "You're sure you want to go first?"

"You bet."

Harrington cleared his throat. "One small detail . . . for all of you swimming the river. You'll have to strip down, boots off, too. Half of that flood water is silt. If it gets in your clothes, it'll sink you straight to the bottom."

Rain's jaw dropped. "Go across nekkid?"

Harrington hid a smile. "Not quite. Tie your boots and outer clothes to your saddle. I assure you, there won't be anything said about impropriety."

"What's that?"

"Your lack of clothing. And think on this. Drowning isn't the most pleasant way to go."

"If we got to do it, we got to," Ellis said. "Only thing is, I don't swim."

"Once you're in the river get off and hold onto your stirrup. The horse can't swim with you on him, but he'll get you across otherwise. Just stay upstream or grab hold of his tail."

"You can count on it. And tonight we'd better double up on watch. Those cattle ain't restin' too easy. Seems like they know what's coming."

Chapter Thirty-Two

The morning dawned cloudy, with a sharp wind out of the west, and it was obvious to them all that the river had risen by several feet overnight.

"No time to waste," Harrington said to Joanna and Tino who was hobbling on his crutch. "We'll get you across now."

She felt she was abandoning them, sailing to safety, while the men took their lives in their hands, but the decision had been made for her.

"You don't have to do this . . . risk yourself. You could cross with me," she said to Angus, although she knew what his response would be.

Regardless of his feelings about the river, he wasn't a coward. Hell, the McLeod hadn't been born who'd back out of a tight spot to save his own skin and leave his men to fend for themselves. "And what kind of a man would that make me?" he asked her.

In spite of her misgivings, she felt a flash of admiration. "Take care, then," she whispered. "Promise."

He bent and kissed her gently. "I'll nae drown today, lass. Count on it. But I'd like you to hold onto my watch. No sense getting it full of sand." He reached into his pocket and handed her the ornate gold watch that had belonged to his grandfather. "Mind you keep it safe now," he said with a smile.

Her fingers closed around it. If anything happened, this was what she'd have — this inanimate object that ticked steadily in her palm.

"Joanna!"

"Coming!" With a stifled sob she turned, ran for the wagon, and scrambled up on the seat beside the Colonel, who was holding the reins.

"He'll be fine," he said, reading her face.

She didn't answer. She couldn't think of a thing to say.

The steamer, *Mohave*, was waiting at the landing, twin stacks belching smoke, and Polhamus was pacing the deck. Seeing them, he came swiftly across the rude gangplank.

"You're early. Good. Let's get that wagon aboard." He stretched a hand to Joanna. "A pleasure, Missus O'Keefe. I've heard all about you. We'll get you across in good shape, and your cattle, too."

His handshake was firm, his face ruddy under his white beard, and she took confidence from his no-nonsense attitude. "I'm sure you will," she said graciously.

"She's always tricky, this river. Sometimes worse at low water than in flood, if that makes you feel better." He cast an assessing eye upstream. "Best come on board now, and we'll cast off before those mules figure out they're taking a trip."

Joanna gripped the railing with both hands, feeling the thrust of the engine, the vibration of the boat as it fought against the current.

"I think I'd rather swim it," she muttered to Harrington who had come to stand beside her.

Of course, she would. It was the way she was made, never taking the easy way, never turning back, taking her fences clean like a good Thoroughbred. "We're doing our best to keep you safe, my dear," he said. "As I told you long ago, you're too valuable to lose."

She jammed her hat tighter on her head. "So are those men."

"Of course, but they know what they're doing and are prepared to take risks." He pointed downstream. "Look there.

219

That's where they'll cross. And Isaac's Indians are lined up, waiting."

About thirty men armed with stout poles stood on the bank beside small skiffs. They were naked except for ragged trousers. A few had brightly colored cloth turbans wrapped around their heads; the others appeared to have their hair thickly coated with red mud, and the sight of them aroused her curiosity.

"Why do they do that? I bet it's uncomfortable."

"Lice," he said.

Horrified, she looked at him. "Really?"

"So I've been told. I suppose there are very few lice that could survive under that."

She resisted the impulse to scratch her own head. "You're trying to distract me."

He bowed slightly. "Of course. And look, there's Jack Mellon with the *Gila* already in place. The two steamers will block much of the way, and those Indians with their boats and poles will keep the cattle from getting caught in the paddle wheels."

The possibility of danger from the wheel hadn't occurred to her, but a quick glance aft proved the truth of his statement. An animal — or a man— swept into the mighty blades would be trapped, cut to pieces, pushed down into the thick brown river.

She gripped the railing harder. "This whole thing was crazy from the first."

"And we all agreed to it. No, Joanna, it's a splendid undertaking, and you can put your faith in our boys and Isaac's Indians. They swim like fish, they know this river, and they've done the same thing before. By evening, we'll all be on the other side, celebrating."

"How can you stand there and be so calm? So accepting?"

He raised an eyebrow. "How? I've lived a long time. I've seen men die . . . and women, too. Some for ideas far wilder and more hopeless than this. I've loved . . . and lost those whom I've loved. We take chances in this world, my dear, and this is one. But, I have the feeling we'll succeed. Only a feeling, but I've learned to trust myself and in the ability of the men I know. In time, you'll be the same, I have no doubt. For the present . . . we wait. And pray, if you like. Prayer helps, you know, even if you have doubts about God."

"I've always believed God helps those who help themselves."

"Me, too. And here we are across. Not as bad as you expected, was it?"

"Not with your company," she said with a final glance at the powerful paddle wheel. "I guess I shouldn't let myself imagine so much."

He offered her his arm and, when she took it, laid his free hand over hers. "A sign of intelligence, although I've never had reason to doubt yours, my dear."

She sneaked a quick glance at him through her lashes. It almost seemed as if he were about to make a declaration, even though he knew how it was between her and Angus. And at such a time! He was her friend, nothing more. Had she never met Angus, perhaps something might have happened between them, but it was too late for that. At the thought of Angus, she quickened her pace.

"Thank you for everything you've done," she said. "We'd never have made it this far without your advice and your help. And now I'm going to do what you said. I'm going to pray, and pray hard."

The first bunch of steers had been cut out and driven to the riverbank. Rain drew up and sat for a minute, studying

221

the current. Even as he watched, the water rose, swirling around Nighthawk's hoofs, making the big horse dance. Behind them, Rupert, the lead steer, also seemed to be assessing the challenge, moving his massive head slowly from side to side, scenting danger, sensing what was required of him.

Rain uttered a silent prayer, then turned. "Let's move 'em!" he called, and urged his horse into the flood.

The edge dropped off sharply. When the animal plunged and began to swim, he slipped off on the upstream side, clutching the stirrup. Christ, it was cold! Colder than a snowbank in December! He kicked out with his legs. *Keep moving. Keep your head out and your mouth shut. They were right about one thing . . . this water's half mud. One swallow, and I'll puke, and those cows'll push me down and beat me to death. Jesus, this is worse than a stampede.* He was being pushed six ways at once, and the water churned like thunder. Or maybe it was the noise of two hundred and fifty steers swimming for their lives. Or was it the paddle wheels slowly turning?

The horse swerved in mid-stream, and his grip on the stirrup slipped. *Lose that, lose everything. Damn the river! Damn my big mouth, saying I'd do this damn' fool stunt. Kick! Kick, for Christ's sake!* He couldn't see for the water and mud in his eyes. How much farther? He kicked again and regained his hold on the stirrup that had turned slippery. If he looped his arm through it? He made an instant decision. He could get dragged that way. He'd seen a man die getting dragged. By a leg, but still. Damn it, his fingers were cold. How much farther was it? He squinted through the pain in his eyes, and then Nighthawk hit solid ground and lunged onto the shore.

It was awkward, mounting from the wrong side in sopping underwear, but he did it fast, sensing the wedge of cattle coming, and behind them Chapo, swimming like a muskrat, holding to his own horse's tail.

"Remember when we dared each other to swim the loch?" John stood, one hand on Angus's bare foot, looking at his brother in the saddle.

"Aye. And 'twasn't much colder than this." His horse danced. He could feel its heart beating in time with his own. "But, for sure, I never thought I'd be doing it in America."

"Nor did I." John stepped away as he caught Scotty's signal. "Go safely."

"That I will. And you, too."

Scotty was already swimming, followed by a sea of heads and horns. Angus pushed the recalcitrant drags into the water and went in after them. No, he'd never imagined this — frigid, turbulent red water, the clatter of horns, the whir of paddle wheels, and a bunch of shouting red men, standing up in small boats as insubstantial as leaves, beating the river with sticks.

The current was stronger toward the middle, and he felt his horse fighting against it, knew the animal's panic as if it were his own. "Easy," he called to it, "easy, now." He got a mouthful of the stuff for his concern. And then he was choking, struggling for breath, for his life, for Joanna who waited on the far side. How much longer could he hold on, needing to breathe? He'd promised her, and a McLeod never broke a promise, even if he died in the keeping of it. The horse hit the bank with a grunt, and he let go his hold and lay there face down in the trampled mud and weeds.

Joanna leaped from the wagon seat and ran. He was lying so still. She tripped and slipped down the bank, landing on hands and knees beside him.

"Angus. Love. . . ."

He moved, pushed himself up, coughing out water. "I

swallowed half the river, but I made it. Like I promised."

"And we're never doing this again. Never, never!"

"Chain me to the house, if I suggest such a thing."

She helped him to his feet, then laughed hysterically. "Look at you. You look like those Indians. Come, get some dry clothes."

"When we've finished. But I need my boots. See if you can't catch the horse."

He was stubborn. And full of male pride. And because of it she felt pride, too, for this man who loved her. She crawled up the bank and found the horse grazing on a willow.

"Come on, son. Rest period's over." She picked up the loose reins and led it back, watched as Angus sat and pulled on his boots over wet socks, resisting the urge to bathe his face, doctor the bruise she saw on his cheek. He'd not let her fuss. Not while there was work to do.

"I'll build up the fire. When this is over, at least you can all get warm and have a decent meal."

That was what women did. Stand by, do chores, be ready with food, clothes, blankets, loving gestures that spoke more than any words.

Ellis watched as the river continued to rise. You could hear it muttering to itself, gathering strength as it climbed the banks, undermined them, and swept great chunks away. Ellis could hear it. Trouble coming closer. Like the whistle of the train. Well, he'd beat trouble that time, and he'd do it again. He rode after the steers that were already in the water. Belly deep, his horse shied, attempting to go back to land and safety.

"No you don't!" Ellis hauled him around. Without boots and spurs, all he had was the strength of arms and shoulders, the determined force of his body, which the frightened animal resisted, throwing its head, attempting to rear. "You think you gonna win this, but you ain't!" he shouted at it, and brought a fist down between the horse's ears. Then it plunged in, still fighting him until it hit deep water and began to swim.

Now he had to get off. Now he, too, had to swim for it, trusting the panicked animal to head for safety. He knew it was a mistake as soon as the cold water took him, as soon as the horse headed for the boats, blinded by its own fear. He saw it then — his life, his hopes, dreams and accomplishments — just the way they said you did before you died, before the Indians beat the horse away and he lost his grip and went down, straight to the bottom like a stone. Hoofs beat madly over his head. He pushed himself away and up, burst out gasping for a breath, just one. Then he sank again into the dark.

They brought him into camp on a makeshift stretcher — four solemn-faced Yumas followed by Deering.

"Who? What?" Joanna ran to meet them, scattering the biscuits she'd been making, stopping dead as she saw Ellis, unmoving.

"Is he . . . alive?"

"I'm not sure." Deering bent over and felt for a pulse. His friend, his link to his youth, the only man he'd ever trusted with his life, and he'd killed him with a crazy dream, just like he'd killed his child, that little, laughing embodiment of everything he'd ever wanted. Land! Cattle! Money! *Greed,* he thought miserably. *I wanted it all, God help me.*

"What happened?"

He looked up, and Joanna saw the sorrow in his eyes. "Damn' horse took an ignorant fit. Horse is dead. Got caught in the wheel. These Indians pulled Ellis out. Just jumped in and got him." And he'd hated Indians from the first. He swallowed hard. "Good men."

But there was a pulse. She felt it, faint under her fingers. "Get blankets," she said. "All you can find. And bring him over by the fire. He's cold as ice, but he's not dead. How much did he swallow?"

"Enough."

"Think anything is broken?"

Deering shook his head. "I couldn't tell. It's possible that damn' horse kicked him."

"Or he could've hit his head on something. Get him into dry clothes, then we'll have to wait and see."

She turned back to the biscuits that had been ruined in the mud. Injury. Death. Murder. The god-damned river, and a bunch of no-good bawling cattle that were supposed to insure the future. Except there might not be any future for Ellis, only a grave out here on the bank of the river that had tried to claim him. She had thought that once the barrier had been crossed they would celebrate, toast themselves, look ahead to trail's end. Instead, they sat in silence, or went about their chores in slow motion, conscious that Ellis lay without moving under the blankets.

Deering sat beside him, hands between his knees, remembering things he'd tried to forget. He'd lost his first family and had gone in search of another. And because of his own blindness, he'd lost that one, too. Only Ellis had stuck, had never cast any blame. Well, when he got back, he'd try to make it up to Clemmie. That was all he could do. That and sit here keeping watch and hating himself for all his mistakes.

He dozed off and never noticed when Joanna joined him in his vigil, never heard the moan as Ellis opened his eyes.

She was beside him in an instant. "You're awake."

He tried to smile, but grimaced instead. "I reckon."

"Lie still. Tell me what hurts."

He closed his eyes again. "Dang' near all of me. How'd I get here?"

"The Indians. They dove in and pulled you out. That was a while ago."

"I figured I was dead."

"Well, you're not. We aren't about to let you die. You're too important."

She meant it. The warmth in her voice told him so, and the touch of her hand on his forehead. He'd been right about her all along. A top hand. A woman with a heart that didn't distinguish color, or that didn't give a damn.

"Thanks, boss," he said.

Chapter Thirty-Three

From Yuma they swung south into Mexico, following the old trail around the stretch of desert known as the Algodones Dunes — a trail that had been used by the 'Forty-Niners, the Mormon Battalion, early stagecoaches, then abandoned with the coming of the railroad. What marked it, now, were the bones of those unfortunates who had died on it — from heat, starvation, thirst. Bones were buried beneath the sand, piled against the cliffs, whole skeletons or grinning skulls, human and animal, bleached white and brittle as they cracked under hoofs or as the wheels of the wagon passed over them.

Because they were short-handed, the Colonel had volunteered to go on to California, and Joanna was riding again. Tino drove the wagon, his leg propped up on the dashboard, and Ellis had taken his place inside, recovering slowly from what appeared to be a concussion, although he had no memory of how it had happened.

Cooke's Wells, the first water hole on Harrington's map, was dry. Cooke's men had dug into the sand and found several small seeps, enough for the men but hopeless for their horses or for a herd of thirsty cattle.

"How far to the next?" John wiped sweat off his forehead.

"Maybe fifteen miles."

The aura of death depressed Joanna. Men, a few hardy women, had died here and been left, and somewhere their families had waited for news, for a hasty note, a word that never came. And Scotty had found a dead coyote, lying where there should have been water.

"This is an awful place," she said. "Let's get out of here, now."

Heat waves shimmered on the desert, a wicked, undulant dance, all that moved in any direction for as far as they could see. Not a blade of grass, not a solitary tree, broke the monotony, only the whiteness of bones buried, uncovered, and reburied by wind and the shifting sand.

They went slowly, drugged by the heat, the cattle with dragging heads, heavy-footed, stirring up dust. One horse dropped behind the *remuda,* then another, then a third, and stood dazed and trembling.

Joanna turned back to them, and Juan called out: "Leave them, *señora.*"

"But I can't!" They were her charges, her children, and they were suffering. Even her little buckskin was moving with deliberation, although she had shared her own precious water with him earlier, pouring a mouthful into her hat and offering it to him.

"We can't stop for them. You understand?"

"They'll die out here! Like those others!" she shouted hoarsely around the dryness of her throat.

"We must think of the rest," he said sadly, for he, too, recognized tragedy and accepted it.

And if there was no water at Alamo Mocho, what then? How could they go on, how long could any of them endure?

The trail curved around a pile of black rock. Looking back for one last glimpse, Joanna saw one horse go down on its knees and rest its head in the sand. Five horses done for, and who knew how many steers. She'd lost count. They'd slaughtered one for food and then fought off the flies that came out of nowhere, lured by the scents of blood and death. Far ahead, distorted by her tears and the rippling waves of heat, she saw Chapo, who had ridden ahead. He was waving his hat in a wide circle, and with a leaping of hope she went to meet him.

"Water! But too small to drink all at once. You go, *señora*, and the chuck wagon. The rest of us will come slowly."

There was, indeed, water. A small depression in the earth at the foot of a strange cliff of many-colored clay. She lay on her stomach, drinking deep, then, guiltily, got up and carried a cup to Ellis.

"It ain't the Colorado, but it's wet," he said with a grin.

"I don't know whether to be glad or sad. There's never a happy medium. We're either drowning or dying of thirst."

"Better get them horses watered and out of here before the cattle come." He drained the cup and grinned again, white teeth flashing. "You're a real lady, Missus O'Keefe, and I thank you again for all you done."

Lady? She hadn't thought of herself as a lady in what seemed like forever. Maybe she never had. What was a lady, anyhow? She picked up the cup. "I guess that's a compliment, so, thanks."

"You bet it is. The way I see it, a lady takes care of everybody else before herself, human or animal, black or white, don't make no difference. You done that without even thinkin' about it, and that's why I say what I say. I've been pleased to ride with you, and that's a fact."

"And riding with you has been an education. If you ever need a job, come to me," she said, attempting to hide her real embarrassment.

"I couldn't do that," he said. "Mister Deering, he needs me, though he don't know it."

She remembered how Mellen had sat watching over his friend, his face a map of sorrow. "I think he does," she said. "I think he does. Now I'd better go help Juan. You call, if you need anything."

Outside, she was glad she'd gotten to the water before the *remuda*. The thirsty horses had trampled the edge of the small spring and turned the water into mud. Fortunately, she and Tino had managed to fill one of the barrels.

"Think that'll hold us till we get to more water?" she asked.

He shrugged. "That depend on where the water is. If too far . . . well, we wait and see, eh?"

She was tired of waiting, tired of the trail that never ended, just kept stretching farther and farther west. What of the men from Texas who'd done this every year, year in and year out, without fail, some of them trailing cattle all the way to Canada? What of them? Hadn't they ever despaired, been hesitant to start out, knowing what lay ahead?

"Come on," she said. "Let's get settled and start supper."

Fortunately, they'd carried a small supply of firewood. A look around convinced her that it had been a wise decision. "Alamo means cottonwood," she said to Angus, when she sat down beside him to eat. "But there's not a tree for a hundred miles."

"Maybe someone saw a mirage here once." He'd spent the last days envisioning lakes of water that disappeared just as he approached.

"Hateful place." Her shoulders drooped from the memory of horses suffering, dying a slow and dreadful death.

"It can't be much farther," he said in an effort to cheer her. "Perhaps a hundred miles."

"And how much more stock will we lose? We'll be lucky, if we have anything to sell by the time we get out of here."

Ellis, who had climbed out of the wagon and was sitting a short distance away, gave her a concerned look. "That's no way for the boss to be talkin'."

"Why, Ellis!" she said, startled.

231

"You heard me. You're the heart of this outfit. You can't quit on us . . . now we're nearly there."

"It's hard."

"Yes'm. But you done worse than this."

No, she thought, *it's harder to watch animals die than to commit murder.* She gave him a grudging smile. "If you say so."

"I do. And while we're talkin', I ain't ridin' another day in that wagon. If the heat don't get me, the flies will."

"How's your head?"

"I reckon I'll live."

"You gave us quite a fright." Mellen fished in his pocket for a cigar, then realized he'd smoked his last one in Yuma. "You're sure you're all right?"

Ellis chuckled. "You'd be fine, too, if you'd been in there with them flies that thought I was a side of beef."

John felt a weight lift from his shoulders, listening to the banter. With Ellis back, they'd get through this corridor of hell. He picked up a handful of sand and watched as it sifted through his fingers. Time was passing. And Francesca — what was she doing now? Had she forgotten him in her round of Christmas and New Year's parties?

"Can I ask you something?" he said to Harrington. "In private?"

"About time we talked," the Colonel said. "I thought you'd never get around to it."

John bit down on the stem of his empty pipe. "You know?"

Harrington stood. "Let's walk. And let me say, I'm not so old I've lost the use of my eyes. Of course, I knew. So did everybody else, unless I'm mistaken."

For the second time in the span of a few minutes, trouble seemed far away. "And you don't mind? It's all right with you?"

Harrington put his arm around John's shoulders. "If I'd

232

minded, I'd have put a stop to it before now. Just treat her as she deserves. She's all I have left."

"You've got my word on it," he managed to get out. "She'll never want . . . for anything, if I can help it."

Always the businessman, Harrington stopped and bent down to draw a rough map in the sand. "With a little planning and foresight, we might be able to connect our holdings. I've been thinking about it. We could preëmpt this part of the valley." He drew a circle. "And, perhaps, file claims . . . here and here." He drew adjoining circles next to the first. "What do you think?"

John blinked in amazement. How simple it seemed! He'd be the biggest rancher in the county — he and Angus and Joanna. And Francesca, who'd somehow brought this miracle about.

"My God, man. . . ." He wanted to shout. To dance. To tell about his good fortune.

Harrington read his thoughts. "Time enough for discussion, when we get to Warner's Ranch. There's fine grass and water there, and I suggest we lay over for a week. Put some weight on the cattle. This isn't the time or the place to make decisions. And I have a hunch Joanna has a card or two to play."

"She does?" As always, any credit given to Joanna perplexed him.

"She's years ahead of us at times. Has a mind like a bear trap. You'd do well to listen to her more often."

"Aye. Well . . . it's hard. I'm nae used to women like her. Women with notions."

The Colonel dusted his hands. "Better get used to it. Soon you'll have two of them."

Francesca. The thought of her was sweet. And she was nothing like Joanna. Or was she?

233

Chapter Thirty-Four

Without any warning, cattle and horses broke out of a walk and began to run, startling the riders, passing the lumbering chuck wagon, spreading out across the sand in crazed flight.

"Let 'em run!" Scotty, in the lead, shouted. "They won't run long."

Joanna and Juan had been swept up in the charge and were the first to understand what he meant, when they topped a small rise and saw a lake, blue, tranquil, surrounded by grass and ancient mesquites.

"What on earth!" she exclaimed, when they stood at the edge, their horses knee-deep and drinking. "This isn't on the Colonel's map."

"A *milagro, señora*. Who can say why?"

A miracle, indeed, she thought, as the rest of them caught up.

"I've heard rumors of such a lake, but didn't believe it," the Colonel said. "Perhaps it has to do with the flooding on the Colorado."

"I don't know, and I don't care, long as it's here." Scotty gave a satisfied grin. "This'll see us through quite a ways."

The water was clean and sweet, the grass at its edges lush, and they moved out the next day content, ignorant of what still lay ahead.

The Carrizo Corridor, a winding, narrow trail through sand and gravel, mountain-bordered, as desolate as the moon, pointed west. Rocky cliffs trapped the heat, sand reflected the sun, and again bones were scattered everywhere, mute relics of despair.

Out in front, Tino's mules labored through the deep sand, and he talked to them in a mixture of languages, not caring what he said or how, but offering his own pathetic encouragement that bordered on prayer.

"Basta! Basta! Tutto é finito! No more will I do this foolishness. *Sono matto. Sono fesso.* I am crazy. Stupid to be here with the bones of the dead. God forgive me. Forgive us all. Pull harder! Yes, you. Hup! Hup! *Bene."* And then, at last, he fell silent, holding the reins loosely in his gnarled hands, trusting the mules to go on without encouragement.

The trail twisted, ascended, narrowed so the cattle had to walk three abreast, heads down, hoofs burning, the clatter of horns echoing the sound of the bones underfoot. Years later, Joanna would remember that sound — and the heat of the march — would taste the sand that clogged her nose, scratched her throat, a taste not of earth but salty, like the sea that had once covered this desolation before it vanished, leaving no trace.

Fifteen miles. The Corridor was only fifteen miles, but they might as well have been five hundred. No one could endure this for long. Under her the buckskin tripped, picked himself up, and went on. Sweat dried on his bright coat, turning it gray, drying as quickly as it appeared, even as her own sweat dried, until at last there was no more, until their bodies had given up their last portion of water, and they were merely dry leaves, skin over bone.

They passed a sulfurous spring, its fumes heavy in the still air — water of no use to anyone except the occasional bird, the sidewinders that left looping designs that disappeared beneath what seemed to be the rotten stumps of long-gone trees.

"Given up the ghost like the rest," John muttered to Mellen. "Hell on earth is what it is."

Mellen shifted the pebble in his mouth to the other side before answering. "I've always believed that we carry hell with us. Make our own hells out of blindness or stupidity. Lately, I haven't seen much to make me change my mind. But they say Warner's Ranch is as close to paradise as you'll find."

"Seeing is believing."

"So it is." He worked the pebble with his tongue, then spat it out. "Even that's no good out here."

"Haven't you noticed?" John slumped lower in the saddle in an unconscious attempt to avoid the afternoon sun. "Out here, everything comes down to two things. The will to live and the strength to do it."

The trail grew steeper. They were in a narrower cañon now, and for a long while they rode without speaking. Then Mellen blinked and rubbed his eyes, blinked again.

"Bless me, I think we're out of this. Look there."

The cañon mouth opened onto a valley, and at the far side were willow trees, stunted but green, surrounding small pools of water.

"Hallelujah," Mellon said, to which John added a heart-felt: "Amen."

"There's a full moon tonight, and it beats all heck out of that sun," Ellis said, casting a practiced eye at the herd. "We oughta keep going. Can't be much farther."

Harrington pulled the map out of his pocket. It was cracked now, and brittle along its creases. "It isn't too far," he said after a minute. "But there's probably quite a grade. At least we'll have light to see by."

Gingerly, Joanna touched her nose. It was red and would

236

probably blister like the rest of her face. Tanned as she was, and protected by her hat, the reflection of the sun off the sand had scorched her. And the others weren't holding up any better, she thought, taking a look at the familiar faces, blackened, dust-covered, most of them with beards they hadn't had time to shave.

It was a good thing she didn't have a mirror. Probably she wouldn't recognize herself. Her clothes hung on her. Already she'd punched several new holes in the belt that held up her tattered riding skirt, and if her face was as haggard as the others' — well, that was one of the consequences, just like not being able to remember what it felt like to be clean. Angus had talked about the hot springs at Warner's Ranch. The sooner she got in them, the better!

The men were all looking at her while she wallowed in her misery. "Did I miss something?"

"We asked if you agreed to go on," the Colonel said with his usual politeness.

"I was thinking about a bath," she said with a grin. "You bet I want to." As she spoke, she felt the skin on her nose crack open. "If we hurry, maybe I'll still have some skin left to wash."

The moon was rising as they came over the last ridge and looked down on the Valle de San José — its oaks, streams, acres of grass, the light so brilliant that each tree cast a dark shadow and seemed to lean into its image. The sweet scents of grass and water rose in the air, combined with the tang of woodsmoke from one of the houses, and Joanna and Angus sat, looking down at the tranquil valley that had seemed so far out of reach for so long.

"There it is. Just like that."

"And how do you feel?"

"Like crying and laughing both together. Like I could sleep for a week." The tension drained out of her abruptly, and she let herself slump in the saddle. No more fighting heat, thirst, exhaustion. No more pushing crazed cattle from one dry water hole to the next, worrying about the men and their injuries. No more pushing herself, when she had no strength left, only the horror of dying and being buried on the skeleton-littered trail.

"And sleep you will. I'll make sure of it. And we'll all lie about in the hot springs like nabobs and watch the cows get fat."

Her eyes narrowed as she watched the herd move past, their horns white in the moonlight. "I have a plan," she said.

"And I'll not listen till tomorrow. Or the next day. Or you can tell me over the fine dinner I invited you to in San Diego. Remember?"

The moonlight turned her eyes to silver. "I do. And I accept. I wonder how I'll feel in a real dress again."

"And will you be wanting a double wedding with John and Francesca, or shall we do it here? I warn you, I've been patient long enough." Almost a year, he thought, and her on the train so proper, so lady-like she'd scared him at first.

She laughed, and he thought it sounded like silver bells, or the clear fluting of larks, and then she was silent, searching his face.

"I've about run out of patience myself," she said finally. "And can we have a honeymoon by the ocean?"

"All the time you want, and then some. The others can do without us for a spell."

"Just you and me. And nothing to do."

"We'll think of something." And how many times had he dreamed it — his Joanna reaching up to him, without impediment, emergencies, interruptions?

238

"Missus Angus McLeod," she said softly. "Joanna McLeod. I'm going to like being that."

Heaven! It was heaven to be clean again! To spend an idle hour soaking away dirt, aches, stiffness, while one of the Indian women in charge of the springs washed her clothes and murmured about the state of her complexion.

"You try," she said, offering what looked like a white jelly to Joanna as she lay, relaxing in the deep pool.

Cautiously, she dipped a finger into the stuff. It was cool to the touch and had no scent.

"What is it?"

"Maguey. For burn." The woman bent and smeared some gently on her sunburned face, then stepped back with a smile. "Is better, no?"

Joanna stretched out full length and let the concoction, the warmth soothe her. "It's wonderful. This whole valley is wonderful. Were you born here?"

The woman nodded. "And my mother, my father. It is the home of my people."

Once her people, and others like them, had had this whole vast land to call home. Once, not so many years ago. Indians. The word still brought terror to many, or hatred as in the case of Mellen Deering who had come as a conqueror into their kingdom, determined to build one of his own and had fought them for every acre, every water hole, and blade of grass.

And that, Joanna thought, was the way of mankind since the beginning. The strong conquered the weak, and were in turn conquered. That was how history unfolded — in change and in the repetition of change. First the Spanish had come, and then the others — wave after wave — a mixture of cultures and languages, bringing with them the end of one empire and the beginnings of many others.

So Alex and John had come, and then she and Angus, and they, too, would have a kingdom, a small empire. Perhaps not so small if the plan evolved by John and the Colonel happened. If it did, a large part of those yellow valleys would, indeed, be hers and Angus's to care for and protect, to fill with cattle and blooded horses.

Behind closed eyes she could see it — home — the mountain barriers spilling down, changing color as the light changed — green, ocher, the darkest purple when the clouds blew up — horses with gleaming hides, and sturdy cattle. And there was Allegra, her child by default, and the others that would come after, born out of love and respect and mutual faith in the future.

Home. And she, Joanna O'Keefe, had been a part of the undertaking, a vital part of a dream that had in time become her own. Who was Joanna O'Keefe? The woman on the train, holding tightly to herself, longing for a husband already dead? The woman who had labored at the birth of that husband's child, who had planned a cattle drive and seen it through, who had murdered a man who was, himself, a murderer? Whoever that woman was, soon she would not exist. Joanna McLeod would take her place, as Angus, rightly, had taken Alex's.

As always, at the thought of Angus, her heart leaped and desire bloomed like a flower in her belly. And that, she told herself, was how it should be, how she had imagined it on that long ago day when she had first looked out over the valley and heard, in the keening of the wind, the cry of an eagle, the promise of the future, the beckoning of a great and lasting love.

Epilogue

Heinrich Schnuth subscribed to the old rule for women just as his father had — *"Kinder, Kuchen, Kirche."* — and let the men worry about business and the things of the world.

His mother had been a shadow figure, deferential and obedient, always obedient, to his father and then to him when he took over the butcher shop and opened a meat-packing plant. And then she had died without his even knowing who she'd been behind her placid face. Not that he gave it much thought. Until today. Until the woman marched into his office and bargained like a Gypsy over the sale of cattle, and then bargained even harder over what turned out to be a quarter interest in his plant, until finally he'd agreed and signed the papers.

His head whirled as he shuffled the copies that lay on his ancient rolltop desk. In partnership with a woman! It was beyond his imagination. But the cash was useful, and she lived a thousand miles away, too far to be an interference. At least, he hoped so.

Nothing stayed the same, but he was too old to change. Perhaps one day he'd sell it all to her and retire with his pipe, his newspapers, his friends whom he understood far better than these young people, these women who demanded their rights, their place in a man's world.

Not only did they demand, but they went out of their way to prove their business sense, like that woman who had stormed in and talked him around while her husband encouraged her with what appeared, shockingly, to be adoration.

Heinrich had never married. He had a housekeeper to see to his needs and a widow he visited on the first Saturday of every month. What would it be like to be married to such a woman, with her new-fangled ideas, a woman who, with a few men, had brought a herd all the way from Arizona simply to outwit the railroad?

Still, she had a point. There was money to be made on both ends. He had no objection to money, only to women who turned themselves into strange imitations of men. What next? What was the world coming to?

"I've married a woman who haggles like a Scots fishwife."

"You've married a woman who loves you," Joanna answered.

"And a good thing, considering the tongue in her head. What next, lass? What d'you want to do?"

She wanted him again — wanted the blinding release of shared desire like a clap of thunder, the sizzle of a meteor. All her life she had been searching for this man who seemed to be cut out of her heart, her skin. She could no longer remember who Alex was or what he looked like. It seemed as if he had never been at all, or existed only as the means by which she'd found her home, her mate, the man from whom she had no reason to hide.

"I want you to love me," she murmured. "Again."

She made it so easy, he thought, taking her in his arms. They fit together like a single garment without seams or rough edges, without any barriers at all. He'd come halfway around the world in answer to a plea from his brother, but perhaps he'd simply been fulfilling his destiny, seeking his place of belonging which was here with this woman in his arms — his love, his life, his bonny lass.

Much later, she walked to the window, drawn to the sea,

the curling waves that seemed a symbol of her own newly aroused passions — that perfect arc before the long, slow descent, the moment of silence before the thunder.

"It's beautiful," she said. "And fearsome like you said. And endless, too."

He came to stand behind her, his hands curving over her small shoulders. So little she was, yet so valiant! He lifted her hair and kissed her neck, and she shivered, shocked at the depth of her response.

"Have you ever wondered what it's like on the other side?" she asked, leaning against him. "A whole new country, a new language, everything different."

He knew her — knew her questing mind, her boundless curiosity, the sight she possessed as if she were part of a never-ending wave.

"Nay, lass," he whispered into her hair. "You'll nae be selling cattle to the heathens. I'll not permit it. We'll have enough to do taking care of our own."

The corners of her mouth turned up in that little cat smile, and her eyes reflected the color of the sea.

"What shall we name them?" she asked.

About the Author

Born and raised near Pittsburgh, Pennsylvania, Jane Candia Coleman majored in creative writing at the University of Pittsburgh but stopped writing after graduation in 1960 because she knew she "hadn't lived enough, thought enough, to write anything of interest." Her life changed dramatically when she abandoned the East for the West in 1986, and her creativity came truly into its own. THE VOICES OF DOVES (1988) was written soon after she moved to Tucson. It was followed by a book of poetry, NO ROOF BUT SKY (1990), and by a truly remarkable short story collection that amply repays reading and re-reading, STORIES FROM MESA COUNTRY (1991). Her short story, "Lou" in *Louis L'Amour Western Magazine* (3/94), won the Spur Award from the Western Writers of America as did her later short story, "Are You Coming Back, Phin Montana?" in *Louis L'Amour Magazine* (1/96). She has also won three Western Heritage Awards from the National Cowboy Hall of Fame. DOC HOLLIDAY'S WOMAN (1995) was her first novel and one of vivid and extraordinary power. The highly acclaimed MOVING ON: STORIES OF THE WEST was her first **Five Star Western,** and it contains her two Spur award-winning stories. It was followed in 1998 with the novel, I, PEARL HART. It can be said that a story by Jane Candia Coleman embodies the essence of what is finest in the Western story, intimations of hope, vulnerability, and courage, while she plummets to the depths of her characters, conjuring moods and imagery with the consummate artistry of an accomplished poet. She is currently at work on BORDERLANDS, her next **Five Star Western.**